A Hundred Shattered Stars

A Hundred Shattered Stars

A Collection of Short Stories

by

Silver Webb

Published by Venefica Lux
Santa Barbara, CA, U.S.A.
www.veneficalux.com

ISBN: 979-8-9891632-3-6

Book design by Violet Sayre. Fonts are Sabon LT Pro and Flegrei. Cover art, "The Fortune Teller," is by Silver Webb.

For Violet Webb, who gave me her paintbrush

and Frances Sayre, who gave me her pen.

Stories

★☆☆

Lady of the Lake

TEN ON THE EDGE OF ELEVEN, the soles of her feet tender and white, Vivian knew about sidewalks and parks, not wilderness. Her father drove up to her mother's bare San Francisco apartment in a red VW van with gold stars and a hammer spray-painted on it, next to a black stencil of a Chinese man in a cap. "Volkswagen," her father said. "That means the people's bus. For Fidel!" Her father wore a black beret and talked about farm workers and political assassinations and starting a collective in the Rockies. Her mother, dizzy with dreams of Jesus, no money to buy shoes, relinquished Vivian and her little brother for the summer. But only the summer.

"If he doesn't bring you back, that's kidnapping,"

she hissed in Vivian's ear, then stuffed a cross in her pocket, sending her out the door with her clothes in a garbage bag. "You're a child of God, don't forget. And don't do that weird thing you do."

That weird thing. Her mother thought everything was weird. Vivian, her brother, and especially her father, who burped loudly as he got in the van and then shouted, "The Republic!"

They took the scenic route to the Rockies. Her father played honkytonk and blues on the radio, driving with a map in one hand and a Schlitz in the other, pulling over to pee in bushes, to clamber up hills just to see the view over the horizon. Vivian didn't understand the new rules. Which were no rules at all. No prayers, no sitting in silence, no confessing of sins, real and imagined. She counted the miles to the Rockies by little cheddar crackers filled with peanut butter, bought at gas stations.

When they got there, it was a cabin of a friend of a friend, in a vast forest of pines, overgrown Christmas trees, forest floor rough with boulders and sharp brown needles. A labyrinth that scared her the first morning she explored. If she walked far enough, she found small cabins housing men who did not want to be found, abandoned shacks falling down, a fire pit with charred bones, from what, she didn't know.

Their cabin was crowded with people, "hippies" her mom would call them, with children named Krishna and

Moon Song. They slept in sleeping bags on the wood floor, ate fish the adults caught, covered with squeezejar butter. With nothing to do inside, boredom set in, until her father said they were going to explore up the road. A field trip of sorts.

So they went up the road with the other kids in the cabin, a feral collection, under a canopy of pine. Air spongy with soil and mildewed bark, turning to something danker, foul even. Rotten eggs. Sulfur. A swamp came into view. A flat plane of lily pads, the pale green of tree snakes, umbrellas for the fish that swam below. The lily pads seemed like magic carpets she might ride, float away to the middle of the lake. In the distance, where the water cleared of plants, a small island beckoned. It seemed close enough to swim to, although her father said it was miles away. Vivian's pulse hurried as speckles of sunlight bounced off the island.

She could reach it, she knew.

"Bet I get there first!" Moon Song, tan as tea, splashed in. Vivian's little brother, solitary and quiet, sat down on the swamp's bank.

"You kids go play." Her father laid on a beach towel with his six pack, long brown hair in waves past his shoulders. He smiled and it was the glint of light on water.

Vivian's stomach rumbled with unanswered dreams of lunch. Revolutionaries did not worry about cheese sandwiches and potato chips. But then, neither did Jesus.

Vivian took one ginger step into the swamp, then another. Her mother would say this place was impure. Cold, squishy rot between her toes, water dark, a snarl of roots. What nobody tells you about lily pads is all that lies beneath the surface, neither elegant nor ethereal. Just muscle and sticky black slime. Vivian slowly advanced, her fingers running along the velvet green pads, flowers floating in the air, like artichokes after steaming, thick petals, sharp tips. She moved up to her waist, wearing an oversized t-shirt from Goodwill. Her long sandy hair dragged the water's surface, eyes an icy blue that made adults uneasy.

"Stop that. You're making me nervous," her mother would say when Vivian looked at her for too long. Maybe her mother didn't like what Vivian saw. The bare apartment, the single bag of brown rice in the cabinets, the thin mattresses on the floor.

Vivian couldn't bear the thought of going back. So she moved toward the island, a place where a beautiful lady must live, among apple trees, she imagined, free of the rot and ruinous black mud Vivian now stood in.

For a long while, the water remained level, and she moved far from the shore, still waist-deep, lost track of the other kids, feet sliding and slipping over thicker roots, a squirming sense of wrong in the mushy silt, a shameful penetration in the squelching. A ripple disturbed the water. A slit of fear in her belly, and she looked back, couldn't see her father or brother. She was alone now. As we all are. Although at ten, there are illusions to buffer this.

Vivian's illusions were thinner than most. The breeze stilled. The birds stopped calling. There was a peculiar type of quiet that came on her when she was in danger, a gaze on the back of her shoulder, pebbling her neck. She felt it now, as if some shadowed creature stood behind her, watching, warning. But she must press forward toward the island. The lady there wished to be found.

Vivian stepped one step further than she should have. The lake bed dropped down by several feet. The water, chilled by the clean current of the lake's center, turned clear. She saw her feet, white and soft, the roots she'd been walking among decorated with purses of toad eggs, viscous and squirming. Little fish like switchblades turned in unison by some secret signal. She sank up to her chest, feet sliding away. The lily pads sunk under the weight of her hands. She slipped down. Her feet and toes searching for something steady, only managed to wedge themselves into a crevasse of roots, now up to her shoulders in the water.

She didn't make a sound as the lake took her under, her face only a few inches below the surface, but a few inches is all it takes. She saw the light filtering through the water's skin above her, thick stalks of lilies shooting up into the air, their blossoms as big as salad bowls, saw oxygen bubbles clinging to the dark underside of the lily pads, and their descent into a nest of viperous roots.

Don't panic, Vivian told herself. It took only a second for her foot to be tangled, it would take only a second to undo it. She reached for the roots, tugging, oxygen dying in her lungs.

He won't save you.

A face floated in front of Vivian now. Pale as snow turning blue in the dusk, eyes and lips the shadowed edge of a glacier. The lady floated, torso visible under a dress of thin white webbing. The lady looked, and saw the whole of Vivian. Lost, forgotten, stomach waning for lack of food, parents on fire with politics and God, Fidel Castro, Jesus.

He won't save you.

The lady smiled, and the pale of her lips turned black inside, her mouth a cruelty. Vivian saw what it would be. A quiet settling to the silt, taken by the roots, consumed by them. By the time her father realized she was gone, by the time emergency workers came, her body would be lost in a graveyard of lilies, a dirge for the drowned sung by tadpoles and minnows.

If you want to live. You must fight, the lady dared Vivian. Teeth sharp in her smile. Nail tips black and razored. Something familiar about her. Something the same.

Where is your blade? the lady asked.

Vivian saw something glinting. A small knife by her feet, perhaps dropped by a fisherman, lying there so long that the roots had grown around it, as if it was part of them. She grabbed it, pulled as hard as she could, until it came loose, then thrashed at the roots around her ankle, fought them, broke them. In her haste, she slashed even at her own skin, a bloom of blood in the water. With a cry, she burst upward, mouth like a fish, gaping, gasping, sucking in air.

As carefully as she'd made her way there, she blindly crashed back to shore, ripping at lily pads, bruising the necks of the flowers, roots cracking under her heels.

She'd always known what it meant to hide. Now she knew what it meant to fight.

"You get to the island?" her father asked, two beers down.

Vivian shook her head.

Her little brother looked at her bloody foot and then up at her, questioning. Then he blinked as he saw the knife.

Don't tell, she thought, and folded the blade back into its handle, slipped it into her pocket.

They never returned to the swamp. And Vivian never

told. Revolutionaries don't cry. Instead, she played in the woods, left alone the whole of each day. She found all of its secrets, its feathers and rocks and small insects, the dried rattle of a snake, mushrooms turning to black tar. She dissected spider webs with twigs, shimmied up the tall trees until the branches were too weak to hold her. She grew dizzy with the view of unending treetops. Looking into that infinity, Vivian wondered if the trees ever felt lonely, to be one lost among so many.

When she came home at night, the adults sometimes asked what she'd done during the day. Vivian never said. This was the weirdness her mother so hated, that Vivian kept her own secret thoughts, her own sense of what was holy and what was not, something hard in the core of her that could not be deceived.

Over the course of the summer, her feet toughened, her skin turned brown from the sun. She kept her knife in her pocket, lost her cross somewhere in the wilderness.

"Your mom won't recognize you when you go home," her father said. But Vivian couldn't think about going home.

A half-hour drive from the cabin, a small town sat on the edge of a lake. A grey pier pierced far into its center, surrounded on three sides by trees. Behind it, a small road boasted only an Old West store with penny candy, although she had no pennies to buy any of those wondrous jeweled things. The greater treasure was the lake, large and flat, the blue of crayons, just enough of a beach to seem like Vivian was back in California, in love with light playing on the Pacific. They delighted in running a circuit, feet slamming against the warped boards of the pier, out to the edge, shrieking, leaping, crashing down to the bottom of the lake, touching off soft plants and sand, then forging out of the lake, to start over again. No bathing suits. Just shorts and t-shirts. Revolutionaries didn't buy bathing suits, although Vivian wished they would.

Most days, they ran in a pack, ruffian children with nobody calling for them to come in for supper. Today, perhaps because it was late in the summer, her father came with them, stayed on the shore, stoned, with a cold beer in his hand. Grinning, staring into space, occasionally waving at them, like they were strange aliens in an unlikely movie he was watching.

Tomorrow was the flight home to California, but Vivian didn't want to think of it. The sky crept up on them, clouds silver and cottoned when they first went into the water. But over the course of an hour, the dome of light above them darkened, fat drops of rain plunking like stones. Still they dove in, ran back over the pier, now dark with wet foot prints, through the thick, warm air, leaping in. Vivian knew when they left the lake, she would be on a plane back to San Francisco.

Her father called out something about lightning, gestured for them to come back to shore.

He can't save you.

Vivian heard the lady's voice. She searched the lake's surface buckshot with rain, shaken by the rumble of thunder.

"You better come in. You'll get in trouble." Moon Song ran back to the beach. From where he sat on the pier, Vivian's little brother looked up at her, questioning.

Vivian saw the lady's face there, just under the water, white hair floating around her like a wedding veil.

On the shore, her father gestured for Vivian again.

The lady's smile turned black. *You've grown wild. Can you go back?*

Vivian's toes gripped the edge of the dock. Dark clouds like gatherings of black birds called her to fly away. What did her parents know of the glimmer of sunlight on water, raven feathers on the forest floor, quicksilver orbs clinging to the underside of lily pads? Nothing. They didn't understand, and never would, the whole of the strange, secret world that lived in Vivian's chest like the marbled infinity of a penny candy. The lady in the lake beckoned, smiling her dangerous smile.

Her eyes were Vivian's eyes.

"Arthur, hold my hand."

Her brother shook his head, remained seated.

"Then, here." She took the knife from her pocket and gave it to him. "You'll need it."

In the silent threading of lightning through the air, Vivian's toes pressed off the dock. As the electricity hit the lake, there was the recoil of a snake, then the water itself aflame with blue fire. She leaped, lifted into a field of light.

Stained Glass

THE GHOST HOVERED in the corner of the room, as she did every night, and watched the woman sleep, breasts rising with the wheel of breath, scarlet hair snaking over the sheets.

"Come out, darling, come to see me." Sleep cottoned the dreaming woman's mouth, made taffy of her words. The ghost advanced nearer, listening intently. The sleeping woman had a name, of course. Sandrine Bisset. Marcel's great grand-daughter. Although it was better for the ghost not to think of her in familiar terms.

"What a beauty you were," Sandrine murmured, her milky face laced with a presence that wasn't her own, a dark halo that would vanish with the morning light.

Yes, the ghost thought. *Once I was a beauty.* A seamstress for the opera, the ghost had been renowned for her straight stitches and wicked curves. Now she was only a few curtains of memory drawn over a windowpane frame.

Sandrine, the somnambulist, sat up, eyes closed. The ghost followed behind her, curious, as the woman wandered through the cramped Parisian apartment in the Beaux Arts district.

"Where is it?" Sandrine ran her fingers over the bureau. "I wish I could remember."

Inside the bureau lay Marcel's possessions, handed down over generations. His medal for service, his pistol, and memorabilia from his years with the opera. A sepia photo of him stood on the piano, performing the part of Mephistopheles. A faded signature, "For my dearest Renata. With undying love, Marcel, 1942."

The ghost's name wasn't Renata. Marcel had signed that photo for his wife, lifetimes ago. No wedding ring had ever claimed the ghost's finger. A mistress. And yet, she waited for him.

"I must do something. I can't go on like this," Sandrine said, drifting back to the bedroom. She sat on the edge of the mattress, her sleeping face wreathed in shadows.

Please, Marcel. The ghost waited, gripped with rising expectation.

Sandrine opened her eyes, the glint in her irises unnatural, slivers of light searching in the dark.

Marcel.

He observed the room through Sandrine's eyes now. The ghost could feel his gaze on her.

You're here. The ghost advanced, trembling. She leaned down, pressed her ephemeral lips of dusty rose against Sandrine's mouth of cherries. An electric charge at the meeting of the sleeping woman's tongue, the tender inside of silk. It was the closest the ghost could come to a kiss from Marcel.

"Come out, darling, come to see me." Sandrine's mouth twisted with the same words Marcel had spoken the night he died. Sandrine tensed in pain, the shadow of Marcel dispersed, banished for another evening. With a terrible sigh Sandrine collapsed backward. Tomorrow, she would wake with no memory of Marcel, the ghost, or any of this.

The ghost observed her a few moments longer, to be sure she lived. They must not use her too brutally or quickly.

I'll come out to see you, Marcel, the ghost whispered. *Please find me.*

The ghost left Sandrine sleeping in the apartment, and walked onto Rue Dauphine. The streets were full even at this hour, late dinners winding into dawn, half a moon hanging over the Parisian skyline. Cellular signals and cross-wires of human desire and bottles sucking hard against corks that would leave anyway.

They always did. Just below the modern stones lay dirt that had tasted the cake-sweetened blood of Marie Antoinette, the viper's sting of Robespierre's ambition. And less distant than any of them liked to think, the metal tread of tanks forgotten underfoot.

The ghost walked the Pont Neuf over the thick, rolling oil of the Seine onto Rue de Harlay. Her heart longed for Marcel and little else save this, the sleeping lady, immense and gutted, Notre Dame. How the cathedral had burnt like a common witch, fallen in on herself, a thousand years of history gone with a careless match.

A match, a faulty wire, no, not that. They destroy from the sky. Marcel, you'll join me here, won't you? You said you would. I believe that you can.

The distant purring of motors came now, sky-laden hunters. Names that bore no poetry. Messerschmitts and Focke-Wulfs. Ghost planes etched an eerie gray in the dark bloom of night clouds. She walked quickly under the cathedral scaffolds. The wood doors a meter thick, immense, immovable. She moved through them as if they were curtains and she a current. Inside, tall stone columns, unknowable miles of midnight in a nave that stretched to a field of stars. Stained-glass guardians stood murky for lack of sunlight, sleeping, but eyes never really did close here.

The ghost would give herself, give her essence if she

could, to something so beautiful as stained glass dim with starlight, the shattered cathedral ceiling giving way to Van Gogh's sparklers above her. All the world singing psalms for Our Lady in flames, in ashes.

Always at night. That's when the Luftwaffe fly.

The alarms unwound like black ribbons, a wailing, toneless mass. *Take shelter.* The ghost dropped to her knees in the rubble. Nothing and nowhere was safe from this. Marcel. Marcel walking home from the opera with her, an orange in his hand, bouncing it in the air, singing *Mephistopheles.* And then the raid sirens, Marcel in pieces, the smell of citrus and mortar rounds. The cobblestones remembered that moment, held some part of him still. As did these stones of Notre Dame remember everything. She lowered her lips to the floor, whispered to them, confessed what must be confessed.

Love has made a wraith of me.

A thousand years of echoed prayers, songs of light and sorrow, lifted around the ghost in the cathedral, flew away like birds fluxing to emerge from the depths of a cave. A scent of oranges, the faded hum of *Mephistopheles.* Then quiet.

You're late. Where are you, Marcel?

Every night, he bid her come out. Yet she never found him. If the ghost could walk through the silent, sleeping glass of Notre Dame, and emerge on the other side, forgetting and forgotten, only smoke, only air. She would.

25

★★☆

Sandrine hurried up the Metro steps, wearing an embroidered blue cloak. Her magenta hair held in place by a crown of glass stars that she'd taken from a chandelier and glued together. A flowing red robe made of sheets and her eyes painted in turquoise did nothing to help her blend in. Sandrine, the thrift-store Virgin Mary, was used to stares. And standing very still. For hours. It was her chosen profession. A living statue of Our Lady.

She opened her notebook, ran a finger over the page that said, "Lucien, coffee, 3 p.m." They had coffee every day at this hour. But it reassured her to write it down, so she wouldn't forget. Sandrine made her way to Café St. Michael, put down her milk crate, and sat at a wicker table on the sidewalk.

The waiter, Renee, poked his head out of the door. "*Café au lait, mademoiselle?*"

Sandrine nodded and drew two oranges from her crate. She wondered if Lucien would remember what today was. Probably not.

"*Bonne après-midi.*" He arrived precisely at 3 p.m. in a Dior suit, gave a quick kiss on each cheek, and sat.

"You look nice today, Lucien."

"You look..." He gestured his hand as if reaching for something nice to say. "Ready for work."

Her outfit embarrassed him, she knew. Lucien cared for the appearance of things; Sandrine cared for the soul of them. She took the first sip of coffee overly hot, desperate for the antidote to another night of foggy dreams, waking after nine hours of sleep no better rested than when she went to bed.

Sandrine leaned forward, determined to be good company. "So, how was it?"

"How was it?" Lucien raised an eyebrow.

"You know what I mean!"

"Well, you might be referring to my breakfast."

"Espresso and dry toast? Hardly of interest." She rolled an orange toward him. "How was she? Tell me!"

"Superb. Like heaven."

"I knew it. Tell me everything."

"You might've joined me, then you would know for yourself."

For a minute, she imagined her arm linked in Lucien's, walking home from the opera, the performance of *Mephistopheles* echoing in the air. They might've compared notes on Margherita's aria, Lucia d'Aquitane's debut performance. But then it went blurry, slipped from color to sepia. She heard the distant call of air sirens, saw dark liquid on cracked cement, something just on the outskirts of memory.

"The opera goes too late for me," Sandrine said.

"Well, I'll tell you about it. Imagine lights streaming

up the closed curtains, a hushed chorus of sound, rising to a near roar."

Her mind flowed with his words, following the story of Faust, a man seduced by the devil.

"It's strange, the opera house," Lucien said. "Time passes, and yet it doesn't."

"Maybe my great-grandfather is still there, singing. His ghost might still be on stage at the Opéra Garnier."

"Marcel Bisset was a lauded bass profundo, peerless for the mid-twentieth century. But let's not be fanciful, Sandrine."

"As you say." Sandrine peeled her orange, tasted a slice of tart sweetness. She'd been peeling one, in fact, the first time they met. *Madame Bovary*, in particular, was to blame. They'd both been reading Flaubert's novel, here, at this café. Sandrine because she wanted to. Lucien to pass his literature class. She persuaded him to see the opera version, and ever since, it had been coffee and oranges at 3.

He went back to describing the opera, laughing, speaking without caution. Now he seemed luminous, beautiful. She saw him in those terms, always, even when he forgot that he possessed any light at all.

This. This is why she cared for him. Lucien free, laughing. Coffee and oranges and opera. Not the controlled, callous man who made a living at Credit Agricole. Who would look at his watch in another five minutes, lie about his plans, and then dash away.

"Well." He blinked. "It's getting late. I've talked too much. Any plans tonight?"

"Just reading at home. Come for tea? There's a broadcast of *Aida* from the Met."

Lucien shook his head. "That apartment of yours...I swear, it's haunted."

"Of course it is. But Claudette Durand is a nice ghost."

"You shouldn't say things like that."

"But I see her, Lucien, in the afternoons by the piano, an exact match to photos of Marcel's mistress. She died in the same air raid as he did."

"Let me guess." Lucien finished his espresso. "She talks to you about him."

Sandrine shook her head. "I pretend not to notice her. She stands by the piano, looking at the portrait of him. It seems impolite to disturb such a spirit."

"Very accommodating of you." Lucien's tone was pointed. "How do you know she's a nice ghost?"

Sandrine's skin pebbled. She didn't know that. Fatigue surfaced, dragged at the edges of her eyes. She glanced at Lucien, felt worry lines eroding her forehead.

"Never mind about *Aida,* then." She swept orange peels into her napkin. "And you? Plans tonight?"

"Nothing in particular. Dinner. Then a walk." His face narrowed when he lied. And Sandrine's chest narrowed with it. He needn't bother lying. It's not as if he'd ever stayed the night with Sandrine. But it was his nature to conceal, control, deny his shadows. As if she could not see them passing over his brow. As if she did not love him anyway.

Today of all days, his company would mean something. At 9:01 this evening, the last day of 29 years would end. Who she would be at 30 wasn't a certainty.

"Almost forgot." He took a small brown box from his valise and slid it on the table.

"Macarons?" Her heart unfolded like fireworks on Bastille Day.

"Left over from a client event. Thought you might like to have them."

Sandrine's spirits fell just a little. Not for her birthday. He'd forgotten after all. But still, a gift. She opened the box with red tissue, two macarons inside, dusted with gold.

"*Merci*, Lucien!" She blew him a kiss as he strode away. He raised a hand without looking back.

She let one sit on her lips, dissolve on her tongue, the meringue light and crunchy on the surface, unctuous and chewy inside, devilish caramel and innocent vanilla, oh, she hummed with sugar, an offering of macarons from Lucien, the sweetest thing.

Renee cleared the table, tapped his watch. "It's 4 p.m., mademoiselle. Time for the cathedral, no?"

"Yes, of course." Sandrine blanched. "Thank you, Renee." She flipped through her notebook. There was no "Cathedral at 4 p.m." only "3:50 p.m. Take ginseng, omega-3, Q10." What for, she wondered? At the bottom of the page. "9:01 p.m. Do something about this mess."

She stood, felt suddenly unsure. She must hurry now before it grew too late. She would stand on her milk crate in front of Notre Dame, eyes closed, and be as still, as silent as she could, imagine light streaming from her, as it did in all those beautiful stained-glass windows. The cathedral. She couldn't remember how to get there. It wasn't written in her notebook.

"Renee?" Panic sparked in her voice.

"Straight ahead, over the bridge." He pointed toward the river. The afternoon sky filled with bombers, propellers like bees droning, the street clapping with invisible boots marching. Margherita's aria reverberated.

Sandrine blinked and the sounds faded, the street and skies once again unremarkable. The cathedral was only a few blocks away. Renee must think she was a simpleton. She only needed to walk there and stand very still. But in the din of a ghostly war, she searched her mind for that other thing she'd meant to do. Something important. Pressing. It had to be done. She couldn't think of it, the day shrinking, muddied, now that Lucien was gone.

★✶★

"You enjoyed yourself." The woman looked up at him. It wasn't a question.

"Naturally," Lucien said from a mattress on the floor of a small room, his spent member covered in lipstick. She was good. But if he built her up, she might raise her rates.

She rose, a spine like a whip, ass cleaved in two by a red thong, the tips of her breasts and the diamonds of her eyes equally cunning. She leaned forward slowly, a performance. Most French women were born with the rules etched into cannisters of red lipstick, embroidered up the back of stocking seams. But French prostitutes took it to a whole other level.

The orbit of the woman's cleavage brought an inconvenient memory of the macarons he'd bought Sandrine today. For her birthday, although he didn't want to admit it. Such things would raise expectations he couldn't rise to.

The prostitute's expectations, on the other hand, were easy to fill.

"Something else you'd like?" She purred.

"I think we can agree, a brothel is no place for impulse shopping."

The purring stopped on a dime. "Make it an even fifty, if you want me to laugh at your jokes."

"That concludes our business then." Lucien set a thin stack of Euros on the mattress.

She swept the money into her hand, as if she hadn't been crawling toward his wallet to begin with, and quickly left the room. Whatever thoughts lit the threadbare utility lines of her mind, they weren't Lucien's problem. He was a banker. He believed in neat transactions. Finite liability. Physical needs met. Like getting a haircut. If his stomach felt cold and numb afterward, so be it.

He straightened his hair in the vanity, distracted by a rosary hanging on the side of the mirror. Perhaps this once, he should consider bending the rules. Go to Sandrine's place, listen to *Aida*, as she'd asked. He checked the time. 8:30. Too late. She'd be sleeping soon, in that odd apartment of hers. If he ventured to her door now, she'd answer, eyes open, but in some other world.

He cut three lines of coke on the vanity, bowed his head a penitent and raised it a god. He buckled his slacks back on, Dior shirt, rolled the tie, and left it in his coat pocket. He walked through the narrow hallway blinking with red bulbs and techno, past a girl of fifteen, experimenting with how best to angle her body. In a sheer bra, nipples like bruised berries, and a skirt that rode her privates, it seemed any angle had its advantage. If not for the black eye. But that wasn't his business.

Lucien emerged above ground, near Église Saint-

Gervais, checking to see that nobody observed him leaving such a place. Turning on his phone, Sandrine appeared on his background screen, sitting with her coffee cup, smiling. He smiled back, in spite of himself. She made him feel as if he were capable of good. But her naivete worried him. She didn't know the rules, that men might have coffee with Mary Mother of God, but they saved dinner and their dirty feet for Mary Magdalene.

His steps slowed as he came to the darkened cathedral. It would be a hundred years before she recovered from the fire. Yet still, thousands of feet trampled her daily. Some mornings he stopped here to watch Sandrine in her velvet cloak, palms pressed together. Tourists would take selfies with Our Lady. Hashtag city of lights. Some tipped. Most didn't. And Sandrine, transcendent with the cathedral towering behind her, a light emitting from her face that had nothing to do with the morning sun. He didn't like to give her that power, even in the privacy of his own mind. It took her into the mythic, beckoned him to wonder what she would feel like, her chin tipped back against the pillow, spine arched, hips asking. He could imagine himself there. Sometimes he did, when he closed his eyes and forgot whose lips were on him. But he would not act on such impulses. Sandrine was something lovely in a world of sewage and greed. And he was more like Faust, in *Mephistopheles*. There wasn't a God big enough to pardon his sins.

A solitary figure approached him, walking through the deserted square in front of the cathedral, difficult to make out in the dark.

"Sandrine?" Lucien frowned. Yes, it was her, walking toward him in a clumsy, hesitant gait. Her crown of stars and velvet cloak, robbed of color, made a dark specter of her. A glint of silver in her hand warned him.

"You're late." Her words dragged. "Where have you been?"

Lucien blanched. "I—had dinner with friends."

"Why lie to me, Lucien, why?" she asked. "Take shelter. They come from the sky."

"What comes from the sky?"

"Come out to meet me, darling. We'll go to the opera."

The horrifying thought came upon him that she was not awake, that she had walked to the cathedral in her sleep. The angle of her hand shifted, and a pistol caught the light more clearly.

"I must do something," she whispered.

Cold washed down the back of his neck. He couldn't imagine where she'd gotten the pistol, or why.

"You're sleep-walking, Sandrine. I'll take you home."

"Let me ask something of you."

"It's late," he reasoned. "Ask me tomorrow. We'll

have breakfast at Place Dauphine."

Her thumb clicked back the hammer. "I have to do something...about this mess."

"Sandrine, no." His gut tensed, primed to punch the pistol out of her hand before she could aim it at him. Maybe she'd found out about the prostitutes, the drugs. Not that he'd ever promised her anything.

"Will you remember me?" She placed the tip of the gun under her own chin. "Remember for me, please."

"What does that mean?" His blood ran with electricity, lungs pained from forgotten breath.

"Is it 9:01? It's my birthday." She smiled in apology. "Yes, I—"

An explosion lacerated the air. Our Lady fell, a curtain of fabric, a soft thud, her crown of stars shattered. Darker than anything, even the cathedral behind her, a lake of black spreading over the stones.

The ghost rose from the rubble of Notre Dame, uncertain how long she'd knelt there. A few days? A week? It was dark still, though she was sure she'd seen the moon traverse the gap in the ceiling more than once. Her confessions, whispered to the floor, had elicited no response.

Love made monsters of us. Yet what choice do we

have? To lose each other completely...

The punishment could not be more cutting. Years, how many she'd lost count, without Marcel. No joyful reunion in heaven. If that's where he'd gone. His wife was there, surely. Renata Bisset was blameless. Just as Sandrine was. The both of them belonged in triptychs of gold leaf and lapis. The ghost was merely the memory of a stained woman. And nobody ever made stained glass of Mary Magdalene.

The ghost walked back to the Beaux Arts apartment, found the small living room filled with boxes, as if someone had been packing. The ghost resisted panic. Was Sandrine leaving this place?

In the bedroom, a man lay on the mattress, in well-tailored business clothes. The ghost had seen him visit Sandrine here only once. After he left, Sandrine sat, silent, listening to music, then weeping, slender fingers pressed to her forehead.

Lucien lay on his side now, slightly hunched, like a crescent moon. Sandrine materialized there, spooned behind him, in her cloak of velvet and gold stars.

The ghost froze. Sandrine was no longer of the flesh. Gun powder glittered on her cheek.

No. It's too soon. If the ghost looked in the bureau, she was sure Marcel's service pistol would be missing. It was the solution Sandrine had searched for nightly. The medicine, the vitamins, even the strange herbs from China, had failed to cure what couldn't be cured, the disease of forgetting. An old person's disease, yet Sandrine was no more than thirty. Carrying Marcel's words had exacted a heavy toll on her. Memory was a killing thing, and the dying of it, too, a terrible way to fade.

It can't be. Not yet. The ghost fought off panic, the silence in the room, the prospect of forever without Marcel.

"You're a murderer, Claudette," Sandrine said, looking right at the ghost. "My mother...her mother... you used us. And now, you cannot. I have no daughter. My line ends. You are alone."

"It wasn't just me," the ghost cried. "Do not say it was only me."

The ghost felt Marcel arrive, a wisp of a shadow looking for a vessel, scattering over Lucien's face, prying at his eyelashes, skirting his lips.

"Come out to meet me, darling," Lucien spoke, his voice startling in the still air.

The ghost exhaled in relief. Somehow Lucien could hear Marcel, could repeat his words. They didn't need Sandrine after all.

"We'll go to the opera," Lucien said, his voice an exact match to Marcel's. He began snoring lightly. Smoke gathered around him, little snakes of Marcel's possession wrapping the man. Tomorrow, Lucien would wake up, take the lease on the apartment, succumb slowly, diminish with time. *Ours. We'll keep you.*

"No," Sandrine whispered, light shimmering from her hands, flooding Lucien, wrapping him in grace.

Lucien sighed, as if he felt her. Murmured, "You were my friend, Sandrine. Truly. I must've loved you."

The room lit with the gold dust of Sandrine's smile. The ghost was thrown against the wall, pinned by the timbre of delicate grace, a sweetness and lush desire in that light, something pure in Sandrine's regard for Lucien, that she loved him so well, even after his transgressions, failures, lies. The ghost didn't understand. She hated it. Why was her love of Marcel any different? And yet, all they'd brought was darkness, all they'd done was drain and use and kill. Marcel's shadow, unable to bear this illumination, vanished. And the last of the ghost's hope vanished with him.

Love made monsters of us, the ghost thought, closing her eyes to thin oblivion.

Lucien shook himself awake, chastised himself for sleeping the day away. He'd dreamt that Sandrine lay with him, encompassing him with light. The cold numbness in his stomach had lifted. He smiled a little at the fanciful notion that he'd finally spent the night with Sandrine. It was just the sort of thought that would please her. He rose and went through the last of her clothes. The movers from the museum would come this afternoon, taking anything that Lucien hadn't claimed. A point in Sandrine's will that had startled everyone. First, that such a free spirit had a will at all. Second, that she did not wish Marcel's possessions to stay in the family. And she'd trusted Lucien to follow her wishes, even when her family said it was blasphemous to bury her that way. The former Lucien might've agreed. But as Sandrine had fallen to the stones of Notre Dame, something of him fell too. Broken open against his will, the cold disregard that barricaded his heart crumbled. A seamstress had repaired the cloak, an undertaker was paid a devil's ransom to restore Sandrine's face, paint her eyes with turquoise and glitter. Lucien had cleaned a hundred shattered stars of their red stain, glued them back together, a fractured crown, laid her to rest as she wished to be remembered. Our Lady.

He placed the things of hers he liked in a box, the little abalone dish of earrings and necklaces, the Lalique perfume bottle that held her scent, a weathered copy of *Madame Bauvery*. Even the empty box the macarons had sat in. He left the piles of notebooks, scribbles of times and dates that were of no use to her now. It was shocking to have found so many, to realize how well she hid it from him, everyone. A little forgetful, yes. Absent-minded, certainly. But dementia? No, he hadn't seen it. Too caught up in his own miserable affairs.

Marcel carried the box to the living room, stopped to consider the photo on the piano. "For my dearest Renata. With undying love, Marcel, 1942."

Lucien picked it up, weighing. A fine piece of memorabilia. The words in Sandrine's will stopped him. "It is my particular wish that no possession of my uncle remains in private property. Let his legacy be borne by a museum."

Perhaps it was time for Lucien to quit humming the part of Faust and give other music a try. He set the picture down. Let the museum keep it.

I wish I'd known, Lucien thought, walking to the door, flipping off the lights. But then, if he'd known dementia ran in her family, what would he have done differently?

"I'd have married you, Sandrine," he said aloud, surprising himself with the words, that he meant them. "Years ago." It seemed like sunlight heated the room.

Lucien balanced the box in his arms, closed the door behind him. He heard the bells of Notre Dame singing, the sweetest thing. He walked onto Rue Dauphine, carrying Sandrine with him. It was almost 3 p.m. Almost time for coffee. He walked toward the café, his steps lightened.

The First
Death

"All dancers die twice, the first being the most painful."
                                                    –Martha Graham

1982, West Village

THE IMPOSSIBLY LONG LEGS OF GISELLE, nimble at the ankles, negotiated Carmine Street with the same precision that had earned them center stage at the Lincoln. Those legs had made Anna Pasternak's dancing career; her turn as Giselle was now legend. Her torso floated above Giselle's legs, ribs pressing hard against skin, head light from black coffee, Excedrin, and two lines. The one thing she could control.

But it wasn't working. No surge of energy, just that

nagging, bone-deep exhaustion.

A small crowd of paparazzi lined the entrance to Our Lady of Pompeii, lazy cheetahs waiting for something worth their while to walk by. The corps girls in the ubiquitous single bun and black sunglasses, bobbed like swans, long necks extended, hoping to merit a photo as they helped to bury that bastard Anton Lalique.

"Anna?" Will Fleck paused in his headlong charge down the sidewalk, clipboard in hand. "Didn't expect to see you here. Listen, have you seen Gregory?"

"Gregory? No." Why did the stage manager for Ballet Minchard care if a backup dancer came to Anton's funeral?

"Stupid junkie," Will muttered. "Carl's out. Gregory dances Tristan tonight if he'll just show up, answer his phone once in a while."

"What happened to Carl?"

"He's in the hospital. Weird sores. Just what we need around here, the plague."

Anna had heard whispers of a terrible sickness in the West Village. Men dying within weeks of symptoms, covered in red splotches. But those were just whispers.

"See you later." Will pushed past her, as if she were a prop.

Anna ducked into a phone booth and shut the door. The lead for *Tristan and Isolde* was the shot Gregory needed. The chance to get out of understudy hell, into the limelight. He'd be the first black dancer to make principal at Minchard. She fished through ripped subway tickets and a crumpled letter from Anton, unopened, until she found a dime and her address book. Three numbers crossed out for Gregory. What had he said last time? Something about Brooklyn being too expensive. She dug deep and pulled out a dry-cleaning receipt. On the back, the last number he'd given her. She tapped the metal buttons, then waited, an endless series of rings. Then "Yeah?" A woman's voice.

"Can I speak with Gregory, please?"

"He's gone." *Click.*

Anna slumped forward just a little, her heart speeding, and yet, she couldn't shake the fatigue.

Not yet, she told herself. *Save it. You don't have that much left.*

Anna straightened to her full height, struck an expression between sorrow and regal indifference, and strode the half block into their midst. She slowed just enough to give them opportunity. *The Daily News, The Post.*

"Anna, any retirement plans?" Only the guy from the *Village Voice* called to her, snapping a half-hearted photo.

She stopped, like the professional she was. "I'm fielding offers from Graham and Balanchine."

"But without Anton..." The intimation was clear.

"Anton was gifted, but he's not the only choreographer I've worked with."

"Heard he was in love with you."

Anna felt like she'd been slapped. But the man's attention cut away from her without warning. "Vassily!"

The walkway exploded with lights. A surge of adrenaline gripped Anna, like stepping onto the stage, like opening night nerves. The black limousine came to a stop, the door was opened by attendants. And out stepped Vassily Dialev, hair in blond layers that draped toward the Bohemian. Face sculpted of rocks and scalpels, a delicacy to his expressions and then all the subtlety of a Gollum when he frowned. Not a wisp of black on him. Tan linen trousers, a white t-shirt that clung to his chest, and a red silk scarf, over-large, draped across his neck, covering part of his jaw.

Behind him, Bailey Hall, seventeen, looking as if her toes had never bled in their satin pointe shoes. She wore an off-white dress with pillowy shoulder pads, hair feathered and sprayed out. She was the new wave. "The Modern Face of Dance," the *Times* had announced. Rounder at the waist and cheeks. Two years ago, the clock had spun to 1980 and all those long, lean lines Anna had sculpted into her body were suddenly passé. Even Cher was curling her hair and wearing spandex.

"What a loss we've suffered," Vassily declared. "My dear Anton. I can't bear it. To dance without him is pointless."

Vassily swept by the cameras, holding the scarf up to shield his face. Anna tensed, waited for his eyes to light on her. His body moved with latent strength, every step choreographed. Those hands...her body called for them, knew the feel of them around her thighs, her waist, lifting her. He was the Albrecht to her Giselle. To dance together was more intimate than anything she could imagine. The side of his eye traced her, but he didn't stop, ducked into the dark doorway of the church, Bailey Hall close on his heels.

"Anna, what are you doing here?" Madame La Reve, a skeleton in a Diane von Furstenberg dress, startled her.

"Am I not allowed at Anton's funeral?"

"There's nothing to stop you, clearly. I supposed it would be painful for you, that's all. I know the two of you were close."

"*Why should I mourn that bastard?*" Anna said in French, so the reporters wouldn't understand.

"That *bastard* gave you your career."

"And then ended it."

"If you say that's what happened, then it must be so." She baldly appraised Anna's figure. "You've kept the weight off. Good. Perhaps Perry Brouset needs a warm-up coach. I'll look into it, if you wish."

Anna had danced on all the world's stages with Vassily Dialev. And now, six months after being cut from

Ballet Minchard, she'd be lucky to warm up 6-year-olds trying out for the *Nutcracker.*

"I'm fine." Anna shook her head. "I have offers."

"Speaking of such things, Will is looking for Gregory. I know you two shared certain interests. Perhaps you've seen him."

Anna colored. Aside from dance, the only interest they'd shared were needles. She didn't like to think of it now.

"I've not seen him, not seen any of you, in six months."

"What did you think would happen? If you don't make yourself relevant, you become invisible. Excuse me, I'm late." La Reve walked into the church as well. Trailing in her ear, Anna could still hear the click of her answering machine six months ago and then Christophe Minchard's voice. "So sorry, darling, but your legs are tired. Anton insisted you go."

And like that. Her family of five years, gone. Vassily, who danced with her, ate with her, told her when to vomit, cut her first line for her, would greet her with a hand draped over her rear, fingers lingering in places he claimed by profession, if not gender, was suddenly silent, gone. How many words they'd spoken a day, how many hours of rehearsal, so many nights they had a salad at Raul's for supper, then he dropped her home at 10 p.m. while he went fishing for bed bait. Vassily was prolific that way. Men, women, young, old...it made no difference to him.

Not that he ever told her. He was exactingly secretive. But she read society magazines like everyone else. Here was Vassily with Ara Gallant, with Andy Warhol. But always, at 7 a.m., he appeared in the studio, warming up his ankles, ready to begin rehearsal.

Of her firing he'd only said, "It's a shame, Anna, a terrible shame. Anton can be such a bastard." And then, silence. Not a word from him or the company. Not a word from Anton, until the letter arrived. Only a note in the *Stage Galleys* that the ethereal Anna Pasternak had peaked with Giselle, that audiences were tired of airy-fairy, that they demanded something more than floating now. As if floating were effortless. It took years of pain and sweat and living in pointe shoes to float like she did. It took only a moment to lose it all, without warning, for legs Anton Lalique thought were tired. *Bastard.*

The pews filled inside the church, a spectacle of flowers on the altar. Anna should go in, but her self-control was waning. She needed a bump, badly. In the vestibule's side chamber, she found the room bustling with dancers, in full costume, *en pointe,* stretching against the wall. Allegra Krakov had her leg flung up on the open arms of Jesus. Rudolf Plachenko in red rouge and Swarovski's, his tights bulging with no shame in the house of God.

"What's going on?" Anna asked Will, who was back with his clipboard.

"We're dancing *Manon*'s third *pas de deux*. For Anton."

"In the church?"

"Sure, why not?"

Tutu's in church. Leave it to Minchard to invoke such chaos. She pressed toward the lady's room.

"Watch out," Will said. "The sugar plum fairies are going at it in there."

Anna steeled herself and pushed open the door. The corps girls were lined up at the bathroom counter, in their underwear, costumes hanging on the hand dryer. Their heads bobbed up and down over the counter, bills rolled, something glistening and sparkling. Minchard ran on sugar plum, their pet name for whatever Will could procure on the street. Everyone except Gregory, who shot horse between his toes, in the crease of his crotch, anywhere that the needle marks wouldn't show.

Susan raised her head from the counter, a dusting of snow under her nostrils. "Anna. What are you doing here?"

The question was getting on her nerves. It was as if, once dismissed from the company, she was supposed to retire to Boise and eat mushed peas. "Is it illegal to come to a funeral?"

"Well, no. But Vassily is here. We know how you feel

about him."

"Do you," she said flatly.

Dawn paused in painting her eyebrows. "You know what we say about you and Vassily."

"Yes," Anna snapped. "I'm aware." Dancers, for all their grace, had mouths like sick sailors. It was quipped all over the studio, some kind of jealous joke. *Anna will only fuck Vassily. And Vassily will fuck anything except Anna.* It had been worked down to *Vassily will fuck anything except Anna Pasternak,* as a way to shrug off his legendary appetites.

Where did Vassily and Phaedra disappear to?

You know Vassily. He'll fuck anything...

Except Anna Pasternak!

"Maybe he did you a favor," Beverly said, looking miserable under a pound of happiness painted on her face. "You know he slept with Carl?"

"What does that have to do with anything?" Anna asked.

"It spreads somehow, right?" Beverly said. "The spots."

The bathroom door swung open and Bailey Hall rushed in, stripping off her dress before the door even shut.

"Bailey is next." Dawn laughed. "Vassily will get you eventually."

"Get me?" Bailey stripped off her bra, kicked off her

flats and pulled a makeup bag out of her purse. "Sleep with me, you mean? He already tried. I told him he was old enough to be my father. I'm engaged to my boyfriend; his career is really taking off."

"Here we go." Beverly groaned. "Nobody cares about that shit. It's not dance."

"He has a gig on MTV. It's really radical stuff."

Radical. Old enough to be her father. Anna blinked. Bailey was just a child, really. With ankles and knees that wouldn't bear the technical requirements of ballet more than a year or two more. And she either hadn't noticed Anna was in the room, or didn't care.

"Hey, careful!" Susan yelped as Bailey squeezed between them and dumped her makeup out on the counter, nearly knocking a mirror covered in lines into the basin. Susan snatched it up like it was gold.

"What is it with you girls and that stuff?" Bailey shook her head. "I have some B-vitamin supplements in my purse."

"Will it make us skinny?" Dawn asked.

"No," Bailey said. "But it give you tons of energy. And extra bonus, it won't kill you." Bailey's eyes wandered over Anna in the mirror. No enmity. No recognition.

She doesn't even know who you are.

☆✶☆

Anton wasn't Italian. So why have the funeral here, Anna couldn't fathom, except that the flower-decked altar and marble columns of Our Lady of Pompeii offered a pageantry that Anton would've liked. Anna wavered and grasped a pew for balance. So tired now.

At the head of the church, men kissed each other twice on the cheek, women jostled for the best light. None of it seemed real.

"Have you eaten? You look terrible." Filomena tugged her by the sleeve until Anna sat on the pew next to her. The company pianist didn't have to care about her appearance as the dancers did. She let her hair go frizzy with salt and pepper, let her waist go fat, and perhaps because she had no hope of playing their game, was trusted by the dancers.

"Can you lend me money, Fil? I'm a little short right now."

"I heard. Staying at the Chelsea."

"Just a ten. Until I get my next job."

"Nobody is going to hire you now, you know that right? I'm sorry, but that's how dance is."

"I thought I had to 40…35 at least," Anna said. She'd lied to the reporters about Graham and Balanchine. Nobody had called. She was two weeks past due on rent. Even the Chelsea would kick her out eventually.

"Everyone thinks they have longer than they do. You have to take it easy, honey. You don't look good."

Anna couldn't argue, so she changed the topic. "Have you seen Gregory at all?"

Filomena rolled her eyes. "He's in some shithole in Harlem, a needle hanging out of his arm. Nobody can get ahold of him."

Soft, abhorrent organ music began. With no warning, Anton's off-white coffin glided by, covered in peach-blush roses. Anna bit her lip to keep herself from crying out of disbelief. It hadn't seemed real. He was a bastard, she told herself, trying to fight off the sickly spiral in her stomach. That white box seemed far too small for a tall man with an elegant mind, a profane humor, and a shattered ankle that had ended his dance career at 17.

"What was it?" she murmured.

"You didn't know?" Filomena raised an eyebrow.

Anna shook her head. "Only what the papers said. Found dead in his apartment."

"Cirrhosis."

Anna winced, wanted to fall away into a world where brilliant men didn't drink themselves to death.

"He's known he was sick for a while, honey. A few years. But he couldn't stop. Said it was his weakness." Filomena's eyes darted to her with a flicker of guilt. "I guess I should tell you. What can it hurt now. He asked me once, what I thought of you. For him."

Anna froze.

"I told him your career was just starting, and his liver was failing; it wouldn't be fair. He insisted he would get better, start a new chapter, ask for your hand. He had plans for you, honey. I'm sorry."

Anna shuffled her fingers, stared at her shoes, beat back the burn at her eyes. "If he cared for me, he had a strange way of showing it."

"What do you mean? He was choreographing *Manon* for you."

"Anton had me fired, Fil. That's a strange way to say, I love you."

Filomena looked at her carefully. "All that time at Minchard, Anna, you never understood about Anton and Vassily. Think back to what happened, the day you were fired. Do I have to spell it out?"

"Your timing, Anna." Anton shook his head, from his customary stool in Studio A. Long corduroy trousers, a button-down shirt tucked in, a straw fedora in summer. Gregory, her duet partner, had looked at her with a question. They both thought Anton was pressing for something that didn't exist.

"Again," Anton said.

But no matter how many times the music played, she

couldn't find what it was Anton wanted from her. He tapped his cane impatiently against the wood floor, the galley mirrors showing corps girls in warm-up leggings sitting on the floor, watching with wide eyes, waiting for Anna to falter. She could hardly blame them. It had been her sitting on the floor once.

Anton exhaled. "That's enough, Gregory. Thank you."

Gregory had raised his eyebrows, shrugged, and walked to the side of the studio. It was only Anna then, standing in the middle of the floor, observed and judged by a million little devils.

"Well, there's only one thing to do," Anton said. He set his cane down and undid the buttons of his shirt, revealing a plain white undershirt beneath. One leg ginger beneath his weight, he walked toward her without his cane, as Filomena began the music for *Manon*.

"What are you doing?" Anna whispered.

"Manon has been shamed as a harlot. Des Grieux assures her that the past will live again. But Manon knows she is dying. Love lies ruined. And yet they dance, to the very point of her collapse."

"I know the plot, Anton."

"Do you?" He raised an eyebrow. "Follow my lead, for once."

It seemed he intended to dance with Anna.

"But your ankle," she said low enough that the girls

wouldn't hear.

"I am not dead yet, Anna."

Vassily stood in a garden alcove to the side of the church. On the outstretched hand of the Virgin Mary, he'd hung a mirror by which to do his makeup. Blue tights, white shoes, jacket embroidered and glittering. She'd come upon him by accident. A yearning in Anna's chest, unchoreographed, threatened to overspill her ribs, like corps girls off their mark, all of her control and pride left on the stage, if she could run to him another moment, leap, and be caught.

But that was impossible. "Once you are dead to me, stay buried," he'd said often enough of allies twisted into enemies in the dance world. And if he hadn't struck the first mouthful of dirt with a shovel, neither had he stopped Anton from digging Anna a grave. Perhaps she had obliged too well by falling into it, somewhere on the fifth floor of the Chelsea Hotel. She wasn't sure now, as she had been half an hour ago, to whom she owed a thank-you note for this treachery.

She'd been looking for privacy to powder her nose, not Vassily. He didn't seem to hear her, so involved was he with his makeup. She saw a crescent of his face reflected in the mirror as he swabbed with thick paste. Cheeks deeply defined with a mahogany shadow, lips rouged in red, eyes lined in coal. His brow was furled as if concentrating for an exam. Narcissus gazing at his own reflection could not be more intent. From ten feet, from three-hundred feet, under heavy stage lights or by candle light, he would be a god, truly beautiful. But up close, she saw the bumps on his skin, the potholes that acne had left him with as a teenager, and she saw something that caused her stomach to go cold. The thing which he was furiously trying to blot out. Mauve splotches near his mouth.

His hand paused. His eye clicked on her in reflection. She felt his appraisal. And a fear that was unlike him.

"Anna," he said stiffly, as if she were a movie he'd seen so long ago, he could barely remember the title.

"Vassily," she said, all of it at her fingertips, the nervous smiles shared before the curtain rose, a thousand times they'd fallen in love on the stage, and a thousand times she'd died at his feet, every breath taken in measure of his. She had given him her arms, her legs, become an extension of that brilliant metronome of his mind. He was called "the diamond" for it, his perfect timing.

He surreptitiously layered another swab of makeup near his mouth before he turned to face her, a curt nod, a sharp smile. He didn't like interruption before he performed, she knew it well enough. But he was too well-bred to tell her to leave.

"You're enjoying your life after Minchard," he said,

and she saw that he'd chosen a different kind of knife with which to cut her.

"Please don't," she said.

"Very well. So, you are in hell, Anna. But you're strong. You'll land on your feet. What will you do next?"

"I've only ever wanted to do one thing. And now I can't."

His expression gave no hint of shame. Perhaps he wasn't capable of it.

"I suppose you've suffered the worst of us, over Anton," he said.

"Why should you think so?"

He shrugged. "You were lovers."

Anna stared at him, crushing inward. Is that what Vassily thought? She wavered. Now that she knew how the dance with Vassily ended, the velocity of the drop, there wasn't much to lose. Except what was left of her pride.

"Did Anton tell you that?"

"He didn't have to. It was the way you danced together."

So he *had* seen them dancing that last day at Minchard. And it bothered him.

"It was nothing." She bluffed. "His timing was off."

Vassily's eyes brightened but then narrowed. "You seemed to enjoy yourself."

"Is that why you had me fired?" She stabbed at him

on a guess.

Even through the pancake makeup, he colored deeply. "Personal considerations have never clouded my work. It's more important—"

"Than anything or anyone." She nodded, familiar with his declaration.

"Besides, why would I have you fired for something so unimportant? If you want dance lessons from an old man, that's your business."

Anna's temper flared. "You're of the same age."

"Who told you that?" The corner of his mouth quivered.

"Your new leading lady. She said you're old enough to be her father."

His expression took on the haughty disdain of a czar. "If you repeat such rubbish, nobody will believe you."

"She's already told the entire company. I've never been the one you needed to worry about, Vassily." Anna's anger fled, her throat constricted, aching to tell him that she would've danced with him at fifty, at sixty, at ninety.

A streak of regret fell over his face, like a shadow from a plane passing overhead. "Please excuse me. I need to warm up."

Anton danced off time. Slightly ahead. Slightly behind.

Jarring. Just enough, that Anna could not anticipate, she must follow and react, must give way to longer holds of the arms, the legs, must snap more quickly in her turns. She was dancing, she realized with rising euphoria, not repeating or reciting or playing back the steps that had been drilled into her. He could not leap or bear weight on his ankle, but Anton made up for it with exquisite control of his arms, his chest, an artistry that went bone deep. Anna lost herself.

Anton's eyes were clear and light. His palm caught her abdomen as she leapt toward him, lifting her up, held there a second too long, the warmth of his fingers pressing into the soft of her abdomen, causing her back to bend deeply, her chest to rise and neck to extend upward. Anton let her roll down his arm; the defeat she felt in the loss of that moment like water falling down into a puddle. She understood then what he meant by the moves he'd designed, the way people will continue to love when all hope has fled.

By the time she realized Filomena had ended the music, the keys were no longer echoing in the room, and still Anton looked over her, hand held. A smile as tired as it was luminous.

The corps girls were silent, their eyes kaleidoscopes of jealousy and wonder. Had Vassily seen? If he hadn't, he would hear about it from them soon enough.

"I have to get back to Vassily." Her voice caught.

"I've kept him waiting."

"Certainly that is a dangerous thing to do. I won't delay you," Anton said.

It was the last time she saw him. Had she said goodbye to Anton? Had she said thank you? See you tomorrow? Or had she darted into Studio B, where Vassily waited, impatient? She couldn't remember.

It was elegant and tasteful. If dancing around a coffin can ever be called so. Anna's body was filled with electrical impulses to move, to stay in time with the music. But she must watch as Bailey Hall took a sledgehammer to Anton's choreography, while Christophe Minchard sat in the front pew of the church and nodded enthusiastically. But she saw it on Vassily's face. The pinched corners of his mouth, the blade in his eye. Bailey's blunt enthusiasm eclipsed his refinement. The expectation was plain in her bearing that he would adapt to whatever she did.

"Jesus," Will muttered from where he stood next to Anna against the back wall. "We are so screwed. See if you can get ahold of Gregory, would you? He listens to you." His eyes wandered back to Vassily. "And Minchard is going to need a new lead."

"Okay," Anna said. "If you tell me what happened—"

"Anton and Vassily were arguing in Christophe's

office. And then you got the sack. That's all I know about it."

Anna watched Vassily dancing in front of Anton's coffin. She couldn't say who had won, in the end. Or what they were playing for.

"Gregory," Will prompted.

Anna nodded and slipped from the church, the reporters gone. She went back to the phone booth, dug up another dime, her hands shaking so badly that half her purse fell out on the ground. "Please, please, please, answer it, Gregory."

"Hello?" The same disinterested woman answered.

"Is Gregory there? It's an emergency."

"We all got problems today. Greg—"

"Gregory has a chance to dance Tristan tonight. He has to get to the Imperial Theatre by 5."

"Lady, Greg ain't getting to the Imperial by 5. He was yelling up and down the hallway all night, said the Feds were coming for him. Crazy shit. Floor of this place is covered in empty envelopes."

Anna's throat clenched. "That's not possible."

"What part of Murder 1 and 2 is unclear to you?"

"Murder." Anna's stomach lurched. "He's not a violent person. He may have drug problems..."

"Yeah, and he's got a .22. Shot his girlfriend with it. She went screaming out into the street and he chased her down."

No, no, no. Not Gregory.

"Does he have a lawyer?"

"A black man guns down a white woman? They dragged him off to Rikers. Gregory is gone, far as you people are concerned."

"He's a beautiful dancer. One of the best..."

"Lady, I got better things to think about." The phone clicked. Anna slumped against the glass, sliding down until her rear met the cement. Anton dead. Vassily sick. And now Gregory, beautiful, sensitive Gregory, put away. It felt like death all around her, a rising tide of grim foreboding that she couldn't save herself from. She aimlessly took the letter from Anton out of her purse and held it in front of her. Unopened to prevent the final word from being spoken. She knew these must be some of the last ones he'd written, post-marked shortly before his death. A little red circle bloomed on the envelope. Then another. Like poppies, she thought, then felt her nose, damp. She didn't care now. Let it bleed. She opened the letter, tearing it when she meant to be gentle, her fingers tremoring. The paper opened and she blinked, her eyes in and out of focus, struggled to latch onto his words, that rolling, grassy script of his that she could only hear in his voice, reverberating in the phone booth with her.

Dear Annanina,

What jackass ever said that the great dancers know

when to take their last bow? A dancer must dance. He will take his last bow the day he dies, not one day sooner. So you have suffered your first death. But not your last bow. That honor is mine. It cannot be long now. An ache in my miserable gut. I can't stay away from the damn stuff. I won't be dramatic and blame it on your absence. Although I've drunk more these last six months than the last six years.

I imagine you hate me now, have heard the story that your legs were tired, that I said you must go. Had I done such a thing, I suppose it would make me a monster. Such trust you gave me, your very limbs and heartbeat. Did I do well by you, Anna who will only fuck Vassily? What ruinous vipers in the nest of Minchard, speaking as they do. Fucking. That is all they think of it as. You never did. That was evident the moment I met you. Do you recall? Giselle? You said, 'To forgive such cruelly as she did, and from the grave?' And I thought, perhaps this one, perhaps she can bring Giselle's ghost to the stage. Do not let anyone fool you into thinking that mechanical precision is the same as artistry. You know of whom I speak. You've learned from us both. You loved us both, in your way. Anna who will only fuck Vassily, but when she is tired and lost, comes to sleep on Anton's couch and eat toast and eggs with him in the morning and listen to Stravinsky for hours, rain on the window on East 5th Street. That Anna. How I've missed her.

You're not the first little bird Vassily and I have batted between each other's paws. Perhaps you are unaware that Vassily and I came up together, were both corps in the Paris Ballet. Had I not destroyed my ankle, we would have been tearing each other down for leads. Instead, I choreographed it, and he danced it. Understand that every time he touched you, it was my mind that lifted his hand, his arm. Vassily is many things, but an original thinker is not one of them. That's why he is called the diamond. Set a clock by him. The problem with you, Anna, is that you are no little bird. We took a falcon into our midst and hardly knew it. I find I cannot choreograph now that you're gone. And Vassily...well, you will hear the reviews of *Manon* soon enough. It will say he is out of sync with Bailey Hall's "fresh young moves." When the truth is that nobody else can give such unthinkable adherence to his demands as you did.

Eventually you will see that it doesn't matter how or why you left the House of Minchard. Although I will tell you such details, if you should knock on my door one of these evenings. Well, forgive an old man for hoping, even as he lies dying his second death. Forgive me my failings. Forgive Vassily his coldness, his temper. He fears aging with the panic of a child, and dances with ever-younger girls, consuming all that he can in human currency, to somehow forestall the day we see, it is his legs that are tired. Personally, I will be sad for that day. He dances like no other. Whatever I love him for and hate him for, and his treatment of you tops both lists, the drive in him is the same as the drive in me. And you. In that way, we are well suited. And between the three of us, something like magic occurred, some dance was made that scraped the heavens with its wings.

Your last day at Minchard was my final dance. I knew as I lifted you that it would be so. Nothing I ever did was an accident. None of our time together was aimless. I've given you everything. I think you know that. Everything you'll need to choreograph your own dances. When I am gone, Minchard will need you, badly.

But a word of warning. Too much sugarplum will burn the heart out of you. And one day, it will fail you altogether. An unpopular sentiment, but humor me and keep your vices to peppermint candies smuggled in your purse.

Let your second death be the one that counts.

-A

Her face pressed against the phone booth, limp with fatigue, so tired of fighting for every inch of stage she'd ever garnered, fighting for money to buy sugarplum, Diet Coke, cigarettes, the little chocolate peppermints in her purse that Anton found charming. Even breathing seemed like too much effort now.

She knew she should dial 9-1-1. It didn't cost anything. If she could only do that, find the will and the oxygen to stand and do it. Outside she saw the coffin being slid into the back of a hearse. She saw corps girls fluttering and dancing around the car, demi-pliés, Bailey Hall on the top of the hearse, *en pointe,* rotating like a plastic ballerina in a jewelry box, and Vassily leaping and spinning with the coffin. Where there had only been a few reporters, now there were twenty, thirty, and the sidewalk packed with couples in tuxedos and velvet evening gowns, opera glasses at the ready, Madame La Reve offstage, grim as a widow, Filomena playing a piano in the middle of the street. Anna's breath pushed intermittently against the glass of the phone booth. For just a moment, half a blink, she saw Anton, standing front and center, the pageant in mad whirl behind him. All for that unbearable dream that what they did mattered. His cane was missing. Maybe that was heaven for dancers; a body that does not decline or ache or break. He nodded to her slightly, tipped his hat. She loved him. Of course she did. Perhaps it would be better to let the flesh slip, to go with him to that painless place, where they could dance together infinitely.

Anton thought she was so strong, that she could and would pick herself up and carry them all forward, find a way to mend their monstrous wounds. But he was wrong.

"I can't do it." She exhaled against the glass. "I can't."

Perhaps Anna couldn't. But Giselle's legs, which had trained since age seven, sweat through ten years of technique and pointe classes, beat out thousands of girls to land a spot in the American School of Ballet in New York, hundreds more to get into the House of Minchard, lived and ached in tape and ice packs, practiced ten hours a day...Giselle's legs were not ready to die. They pressed against the ground, forcing Anna upright. She took the receiver in her hand, stabbed at the numbers, missed, tried again.

9-

Her finger slipped, heart threadbare, mind waning. But her legs would not give in.

1-

Anton and Vassily had been her first death, but she would not let them be her second. Her legs held her up as she reached for the last button, "1" wavering in front of her like the hope of a second encore.

Oh Yes, Dr. No

The thin, dry light of the desert made my head feel like it was floating. Or maybe that was the Seconal kicking in. Sinatra crooned, "Please Don't Talk About Me When I'm Gone" as I cruised along North Indian Drive, the top down on my Roadmaster Skylark. A cigarette lazed on my lip, black bow tie and white dinner jacket pressed. I parked in back of the Riviera, the sun-and-gin-soaked queen of Palm Springs under a crown of palm trees. Sure, I could walk straight through the front door, but I liked to come in the back way, keep 'em guessing. I threaded around the turquoise pool and orange loungers filled with bikini blondes, sucking down the last light of dusk.

"Is that who I think it is?" one girl whispered.

"It sure is."

At 6 feet tall, sleek black hair, blue eyes behind Foster Grants, there was no missing me.

"What movie was he in?"

Okay, maybe it had been a few years since my last hit. The ball dropped on 1960 in Times Square, and suddenly nobody cared if I was movie gold in '55 and '58. No denying I was on the ropes.

But this is the night Mickey Fontaine gets his star back. I just needed one photo to shoot me into orbit again. One picture with Frank and the boys at the Caliente at 3 a.m., dirty Martinis, hair slick with Vitalis. I'd be rolling back to L.A. on Monday with a pocketful of movie offers.

The Riviera dining room glowed with starlets swimming in champagne, studio execs in black tie. The seductive stink of steak cut with the scalpel of Martinis.

Behind the bar, Viggo nodded at me, his fat lips pursed. A bald stump of a man. But he could mix a Manhattan that would make angels take up pitchforks.

"You look beat," I said. "Mrs. Viggo not starching your shorts?"

"You owe me, Mickey."

"Still sour about that fifty, huh? Here." I slid signed glossies of me in *Tallahassee Dawn* out of my pocket.

"These go for a nickel, tops. I want my money."

I kept an easy smile. "And I want a whiskey sour. My messages too, hold the mayo and pickle."

Viggo stonewalled until I put a dollar down, then

he slapped my messages on the bar. I glanced at the first. "Call me, you bastard —Sylvia." The second read, "Meyer Fishkin. Fishkin Creative Agency." My wife or my agent. Well, an actor has to have priorities.

However, the phone rang before I could dial my agent, and Viggo picked up. "Sure, he's here, Mrs. Fontaine." He shoved the receiver into my hand.

"Darling." Her voice was throaty, annoying. "Where are you staying?"

"The Riviera. You're calling me here, aren't you?"

"They don't have a room number for you. You got a place in Palm Springs I don't know about?"

"Meyer is springing for the hotel," I lied. "You need a new pair of cha-cha heels, ask him. What does it matter anyway, my room number? You want to send me a bottle of champagne, celebrate?"

"I'd like to talk with you."

"About what?"

"You know what."

"You signed the contract, baby. Non-Disclosure clause, Page 5. Shut your mouth and smile when they ask about me."

"You son of a—"

I hung up and dialed Meyer. He was the one who mattered.

"Good news, Mickey. Harry Saltzman's on board. They're talking call-back, fly you to London. I need you in shape. Work on your tan. Ease up on the pills.

73

Nothing to rock the boat."

My gut tightened with adrenaline. Landing the Bond movie would put me back on top. "What about Broccoli?"

"Albert's on the fence. Said you're too pretty, asked how Sylvia is."

"Listen, Meyer, about that."

The phone went quiet.

"It's over with Sylvia," I said.

I heard the nervous clicking of his pen against his shiny desk.

"Tell me about Sylvia," he said so smoothly it sounded homicidal. "Albert Broccoli likes those pictures of you two in church. Looks good in *Life*. Understand?"

"Already pulled the trigger. Sent the papers to her yesterday."

"She got anything on you? Anything she can use?"

"'Course not," I lied.

"You got a non-disclosure clause on her, right? Tell me you still got the original."

"Sure I do. Never mind where."

"You pretty son of a bitch, you better make Palm Springs pay. 35-22-35. D-cup at least. You want Bond? Get yourself a girl." Meyer hung up.

I washed my last two yellows down with whiskey. A surge of blood hit my head, lifting me off the ground. I parted the cocktail crowd to the piano in the middle of the room, lit a cigarette, and leaned against the baby grand.

"It's good to see you, Mr. Fontaine." Weimar's gold moustache lay in two pencils over his nervous lips. His face flamed when I looked at him, and his fingers slipped off the keys for a second, then he continued playing "Come Fly with Me."

"How's life, Weimar?" Scanning the room, I spotted a few character actors, but no one I needed to impress.

"Not so bad, Mr. Fontaine, although—"

"That's great, kid. Listen, my headache is back. I need my yellows."

"I didn't know you were coming tonight."

"Eckerd's is open 'til ten. When's your next break? Now?"

"Sure, sure." Weimar's fingers trailed off the piano. He was close to thirty, but looked twenty, like a malnourished Danny Kaye. He limped away, leg riddled with shrapnel.

I ordered another sour, biding my time. Half an hour, another sour. And almost as if Meyer Fishkin wore a turban and saw the future, a 35-22-35 D-cup walked in. Lips red, curls whiter than blond, dress royal blue. The patriotic Margot LaRoy on the arm of a famous shortstop. Her first movie and she'd struck gold. *Angel's Folly* was up for an Oscar.

"Get Mr. Home Run away from the girl, would you." I slid Viggo another dollar. A few minutes later, the valet drew the shortstop away. I sauntered toward

Margot LaRoy, let her get a good look at me.

"Smoke?" I popped my case open.

She shook her head. "If you don't mind my asking, who are you?"

I blanched, then refocused. "Fontaine. Mickey Fontaine."

"Oh, yes." She nodded. "You did the racehorse movie."

"*Tallahassee Dawn*." I shoved the case closer. "Cigarettes are good for your figure, so try one."

She blinked, eyelashes a curtain of disdain. But she slipped one of my Morlands out, and I lit it, made sure she caught the engraving on the side of my lighter. *Mickey, let's go fishing again –Jack Kennedy.*

She exhaled a plume of smoke.

"You like lobster? I'll take you to Melvyn's tomorrow night. Full band. A great scene."

She leaned forward like she was interested, cleavage pressing the rim of her bustier. "Gee, I'd love to."

I still had it, still had the touch.

"But Mr. Sinatra's party is tomorrow. I'd hate to miss that, you know?"

My gut clenched. Nobody had told me about a party.

Margot exhaled smoke from my cigarette. "Tastes odd, like women's cigarettes."

"Balkan-Turkish mix. For my next part. The James Bond flick."

"Heard David Niven had it."

"Get your ears checked, angel."

"I didn't mean—"

"Excuse me." I left her in mid-sentence. Ignore a girl, and she'll trip over herself to shine your shoes. I headed toward Weimar, who was limping back into the room.

"I'm sorry, Mr. Fontaine, it's only half a bottle. Too soon since my last refill."

"There are two kinds of guys in this world, Weimar. *Yes* men and *No* men. Which is it you want to be?"

Weimar looked confused. "A *Yes* man?"

I shook my head. "You want to be a *No* man. You order ham, they bring corned beef. What do you say?"

"No?"

"That's right. Some two-bit bird at Eckerd's gives you half a bottle for your leg full of shrapnel, you tell her no."

"Sorry I let you down." He handed me a folded evening *Post*. "I think you should read this though."

"Forget about it." I took a clean bill out of my wallet. "Get yourself a steak and a Martini."

"This is a dollar bill, Mr. Fontaine."

"So buy yourself a burger and a Coke."

He turned away, shoulders rounded. Weimar didn't have the brass to ask for money for the yellows, and I knew it.

"Meyer Fishkin for you, Mr. Fontaine." A waiter gestured me to the bar phone.

I cranked up my smile, took the receiver.

Meyer hissed, "You seen the evening *Post*? You're all over it. 'Fontaine's Lavender Marriage Quitsville.'"

I kept my expression controlled, in case anyone was watching. "Who fed them that?"

"Who else?"

"Sylvia's on non-disclosure."

"Sylvia's on Seconal with Gin & Sin chasers. She called my office, sobbing, says the furniture is gone. Mickey Junior is sleeping on the floor. Tried to shake me down for it."

"What about Bond?" That was all that mattered now.

"Bond is out. Guess who else reads the evening papers? Albert Broccoli, that's who. Says he needs a ladies' man for the part. Rock Hudson, Cary Grant, someone like that. Now we're talking the part of Felix Leiter for you."

"Bond's sidekick? No way. No."

"You got any bright ideas?"

"Sure I do. Margot LaRoy is on the hook. She'll be at Sinatra's bash tomorrow. I need an invite. You're falling down on the job, Meyer."

"You'll be there. I got some guys can tail you with cameras. I want you ducking out of the party back to your place, arm on the girl's shoulder, breakfast the next day at Keedy's, lipstick on your collar, the whole deal."

"Who says I have a place here?"

"You sleeping in the Roadster now? 'Course you have a place. Take her home with you. Word gets out you lost Bond, you're done."

The cement walk divided two flat planes of gravel, ending in a white wall checkered with cut-out squares. Behind it sat a perfect rectangle of a house, save for a roof that rose up ten feet higher on one end.

I stepped through the double red doors and exhaled. My place. Nobody from my life in L.A. knew about it. This was where I kept everything important. The framed letter from the Academy. The bust of me as Caesar. Memorabilia from fifteen years in film. All of it would be worth a mint, some day.

I poured a sour, loosened my bow tie, surrounded by cubed sofas in clean tones of green and yellow. The world could burn and I'd have the bungalow. Perfect silence. No phone here. I'd rather take my messages at the Riviera and keep 'em guessing. I unbuttoned the tux, unfastened the waist cincher, let it fall on the bureau, which held my photos. Not the kind that make it into *Life*. Photos that thrilled me, and made me just a little sick at the same time. In the drawer beneath them, the will, the deed, all the things Sylvia had no business sticking her nose in.

That had been a low blow, Sylvia shaking Meyer down. Of course I didn't want Mickey Junior on the streets. But it wasn't like he was mine. I'd been filming in Italy with Rolando Rossi when she sent a telegram, *You're going to be a daddy.* The rumors about me stopped on a dime. The press ate the photos up, the two of us outside the hospital, Sylvia wan but glamorous, me the proud father. Until the Roadmaster's door shut and we drove off.

"Can't you keep that thing quiet?" I'd asked.

"Babies cry, Mickey. It's what they do. Being married to you has taught me that."

"Jesus, it was just that once."

"Yeah, but it was a doozy. Don't forget, I still have that letter you wrote."

"So who's the father?" I hit back.

"Meyer Fishkin. Great in the sack."

That's Hollywood, I guess. My agent had a PR problem, so he fixed it himself.

I flipped the lid off Weimar's PX bottle, slit open a yellow, threw in some chloral hydrate, swallowed it with vodka, watched the pool lights go sideways. I thought of my line to Barbara Stanwyck in *Tallahassee Dawn,* "Close your eyes for the last time, baby," just as the doorbell rang. I stumbled to the door, cracked it open.

"Anyone follow you?" I asked.

"No, Mr. Fontaine, I was very careful."

"No. That's what I like. Come in, kid."

Frank's house in Rancho Mirage wasn't better than mine. It wasn't. Standard modern furniture, a line of windows looking out at the pool. My bungalow felt more intimate. It had character. But it didn't have Dean Martin and Sammy Davis Jr. And an even bigger problem for me, this place had Senator Kennedy staying overnight on the campaign trail.

"Show Jack your lighter?" Margot LaRoy had smiled brightly as she passed me in a red satin number, almost as if she knew I'd paid some guy in Reseda fifty cents to engrave my lighter.

The night didn't go as planned. Frank was holed up in the room with his toy trains, the door shut. All the cool kids were in there, along with Jack and Margot. I'd heard someone whisper, "Dr. Feelgood." Maybe Jack's doctor was in there with them, throwing a piñata party with reds and yellows. But I wasn't in that room. In '55, it would've been my party. Now I was left to circle the living room with B-grade entertainment. Roddy McDowall in a black turtleneck, Eli Wallach with a nose like a French horn. I ignored Weimar glancing at me over the piano. It seems Ol' Blue Eyes thought highly of Weimar. For some reason that rankled me.

"Mr. Fontaine?" A maid appeared with a phone, long cord trailing.

"The Felix Leiter part is out." Meyer's voice slapped me in the face. "Afternoon edition has a photo of you with your arm on some pianist. You two looking chummy at Melvyn's."

"Melvyn's—With Weimar? Don't remember that."

"I told you to ease up on the pills. Anyway, promised Broccoli you're halfway down the aisle with Margot LaRoy. Now he says you can play the villain. Doctor—"

"No!" I said emphatically.

"That's right, Doctor No."

"No, Meyer, I mean *No*. I won't do it."

"Fifteen years I been covering for you, Mickey. Take the girl home or we're done." The phone went dead.

I stalked toward Weimar.

"Neat move," I growled. "How much they give you, the *Post*?"

"You kept drinking, taking pills. I begged you not to, but you drove to Melvyn's anyway. What could I do? You're stronger than me." Tears gathered in his eyes.

"Babies cry, Weimar. It's what they do. Forget it, we're done." I walked out to the pool, trying to calm down, recalculate my plan. There would be no photo with the boys. And if Frank bagged her first, there definitely wasn't going to be a pillow fight with Margot LaRoy.

"Mickey, baby, sweetheart." A smooth, rich voice rolled into my ear. "You dig my little clambake here?"

I willed my pulse not to jump. "Nice of you to invite me, Frank."

"Can't say I remember doing so. But have a smoke

82

with me." He was dressed sharp in a blue suit and white shirt. He smiled, big teeth like a half moon, those queer eyes not laughing.

"Sure, Frank." I followed him to the far side of the pool.

Frank lit a Camel. I fumbled with my case, and the Morlands sprang onto the cement patio.

"Have one of mine." Frank offered me his pack. Then I realized, I'd have to light it. The Jack Kennedy lie flickering poolside.

"Wouldn't know what to do with one of those." I laughed it off.

He shook his head like I was crazy. "You're cutting me to the bone, here, Mickey. Haven't said what you think of the house."

"Pretty plush, Frank. Say, I got a place on North Rose. Maybe you and Dino come by?"

"Sure, we have a few laughs. I fly a few girls in from Vegas."

My smile flat-lined.

Frank raised an eyebrow. "Take my advice, either find yourself a girl, or find yourself a nice dress to wear. But leave Margot alone. She's a ring-a-ding broad, deserves a guy with lead in the loafers, lotsa meat in the spaghetti. Understand?"

"Sure." I swallowed.

"I look out for my friends." Frank advanced and I backed up, flummoxed by his closeness. Bergamot and rosemary simmered on his neck. My heels balanced on the edge of the pool behind me.

"Viggo mixes a mean Manhattan down at the Riviera." Frank's tone shifted. "It's not nice, keeping him on a string for fifty. So be nice and pay the man." He pressed my forehead and I tipped backward into the pool, all the way to the bottom of the deep end. For a minute, I thought of the letter I'd written to Sylvia and wished I could stay down there. But my lungs wanted to live, and I burst out of the water, rolling onto the patio like a water-sick fish.

Burly hands picked me up, hustled me toward the gate.

"Are you okay?" Margot pushed her way past the security men. She inserted herself under my arm. "Frank's a bully, that's all."

I was shoved out the gate, Margot after me.

"What did you say to upset him, Mickey?"

Maybe she felt sorry for me. I could use that in my favor. "Told Frank to stay away from you. Said you deserved better."

"Aw, that's sweet."

"Figured he'd fight fair, but I was wrong. Come back to my place?"

"I really shouldn't. I don't want the papers to get wind of it."

"At least help a fella to his car?"

I leaned on her as we walked to the Roadster. Like

clockwork, the camera flash hit us. Mickey Fontaine with his arm around Margot LaRoy. If I wasn't sopping wet, it'd be photo of the year.

I opened the door and Margot slipped in to escape the camera. I took the wheel, eased the Roadster into motion.

"How much was that photo worth, Mickey? You set that up?"

"Pretty sharp for a blonde."

"I'm not really a blonde."

"What's your real name then?"

"Marcy Stolwinski."

I coughed. "Margot LaRoy has a nice ring to it."

"What's yours?" she asked.

"Mickey Fontaine," I lied.

She leaned back, looking resigned. Maybe we had an understanding. I cut from West Regal onto North Rose, and coasted into the driveway.

"It's smaller than I expected." Her red heels clicked into the bungalow. The minute we were inside, I knew it was a mistake to let her see my things. She stopped to read the framed letter from the Academy.

"Not everyone gets nominated," I said. So what if I lost to William Holden?

Margot nodded, her mouth twitching.

"You like art?" I pointed to the bust of me as Caesar.

She ran one red nail over it, and I started to sweat. Sure it was a stage prop covered in copper paint, but it was still art.

"Not too many guys have a Styrofoam bust of themselves." She paused in the bedroom doorway. "I know what I'm here for. Do you?"

"I'll make drinks."

"I only drink champagne." She disappeared into my bedroom. I poured a sour, gulped it, poured another round, and followed. She reclined in a sheer number. This is why guys don't trust girls. She had a nightie in her purse—just in case.

"That's not champagne," she objected.

"This'll make it sparkle." I handed her a yellow.

"You wouldn't be slipping me a Mickey, would you, Mickey?"

"Willingness doesn't seem to be an issue, Margot."

"I don't know why, but I trust you." Her eyes reflected the lights of the pool, and for a moment I understood why the cameras kissed her. She balanced the yellow on her lower lip, let the moisture from the tip of her tongue stick it, then flicked the capsule backward into her mouth.

"Are you acting?" I asked.

"Are *you*? Most guys die for that trick."

I woke, eyes split by morning light. Margot lay naked on her stomach, sheet down to her waist. My screaming headache made it hard to remember what exactly I'd done. I got up, brewed coffee, flaming hot, to get the taste out of my mouth. Found my bottle of yellows, took two for good measure. I'd be loose enough to make it look good at Keedy's with a just-kissed starlet on my arm. My fiancé, if Meyer would front me the cash for a ring.

"Rise and shine," I called. When I walked in, she was just sitting up, her makeup smeared.

"I hope that coffee's for me."

"Sure it is." I handed her the mostly drunk cup.

She shifted her hips, winced a little. "I guess it's true what they say about you."

My stomach tightened. "What do they say about me?"

"You don't like to look a girl in the face when you do it. Flip her over, so you can pretend she's someone else."

"You enjoyed it, anyway." I bluffed.

"Did I? Academy Awards, here I come."

I cracked her across the cheek, sent her and the coffee flying over the edge of the bed. Margot pulled herself up, bleeding at the corner of her mouth. I was used to Sylvia, who at least had the good sense to stay down.

As if I was the one who'd been hit, my knees buckled. I sank to the ground and struggled to stand back up but felt like I was underwater, back at the bottom of Sinatra's pool.

Margot looked at me with the disinterest of a cat. After a few minutes, she poked me with her foot, then nodded when I didn't respond.

"You hit like a girl, Mickey. Weak wrists. Weak everything. Even the coffee is weak."

She took a stack of papers from the bedside table. My legal documents. And photos. Rolando kissing me on the Amalfi Coast. Had she even swallowed that yellow or had she been up all night, going through my things?

My arms were dead. "Why am I...?"

"Check your pills, lover. Not all yellows are the same. Morphine comes in all different colors."

She moved into the bathroom. How did she know I was allergic to morphine? Sylvia knew. Who else? My pharmacist...maybe Weimar.

I inch-crawled to the living room before I remembered. No phone.

Margot came out dressed, as my breath grew labored and throat tightened. Her lipstick was touched up, but the cut was still visible. I could guess what song she'd sing to the cops.

He was violent, drank too much, took too many pills. I tried to stop him, but he wouldn't listen. What could I do? He's so much stronger than me.

Somehow, Margot and Weimar overlapped.

She let a sheet of stationary fall, like a dead leaf drifting down, landing by my hand. I recognized my writing. It was the note I'd left the night I cried in front of Sylvia.

I don't want to live. I can't take it anymore, this lie.

—*Mickey.*

I floated a few inches back from my body and remembered Rolando's mocha eyes asking me to stay with him on the Amalfi Coast. I said my career came first and flew back to L.A. Now I saw Weimar, trying not to cry when I told him we were done. My heart curled in on itself, beating slower and slower.

"No," I whispered and my mouth felt like rubber.

Margot tucked the papers into her purse. "Sylvia figured you had a place, just didn't know the address. She was right, everything is here. Deed to the house, your will, everything."

"No," I moaned.

"You say that a lot. Would've been funny if you got the part." As she moved past the bust of me as Caesar, she flicked it lightly, watched it topple over and bounce.

"Sylvia...murderer..." I choked out the words.

"Sylvia? You're not the brightest guy, Mickey. Never once asked me who my agent is."

Meyer? Not possible. No.

"What agent wants his illegitimate child in the poorhouse and an aging star making an ass of himself? Sylvia gets the bungalow, Meyer gets rid of a liability. If Meyer Fishkin has a PR problem, he takes care of it."

I watched the lines of last night's stockings walk to the door. She paused and smiled. "Close your eyes for the last time, baby."

Scott Free

"DUDE, WHAT'S THAT SMELL?" Bug sniffed the air, then buried his nose in the armpit of his plaid shirt.

"Half-digested broccoli," I said. "It floats up from the bathroom vents on the lower level."

But Bug couldn't hear me. Maybe it was the headphones blasting Pearl Jam. He resumed rocking back and forth, dirt under his fingernails, long black hair stuffed in a beanie. We'd started the ride from L.A. in a chemical cloud of bleach. Ten hours in, the toilets on the first level plugged up, and the broccoli cheese soup the dining car had served for dinner was fulfilling its destiny as a cataclysm to hell.

"I can help you with that." Toby popped up from the seat in front of us, cheery in his waxed loop-de-loop moustache. Side-buzz blond and a tattoo sleeve of Jesus propaganda.

Bug slid his headphones off one ear and Toby held up a small glass jar of something lardish.

"I'm vegetarian," Bug said. "Get that shit out of my face."

"Man-Flower deodorant is all-natural and cruelty free. I went to Borneo myself, to make sure the sun bear bile is ethically sourced. It's consensual."

"Consensual?" Bug frowned.

"Yeah, the sun bears enjoy it, honestly."

"Sicko," Bug muttered, and then, "My butt hurts."

It's true that 37+ hours on Amtrak will break your ass, if you ride the coach seats. No pillow or hemorrhoid doughnut will spare you that. But Bug's ass hurt for an entirely different reason.

"This is what I'm up against," Toby grumbled. Living in his parents' basement was not helping his dream of an all-natural man soap that battled the stink. Thus his first hustle on the Coast Starlight to Vancouver and back to L.A. Although it really ought to be called the Coast Stardust for the amount of smack that hopped on and off the train.

The air in the car shifted, lightened for me, as Alex came up the aisle in black engineer boots, long legs in jeans so faded they verged on white, a button-down Oxford tucked in, and an old leather jacket with a Misfits skull on the back.

"Goin' okay?" Alex leaned over me, as if I wasn't

there, and fist bumped Bug.

Alex's face defined slender androgyny, a punk David Bowie or Tilda Swinton. Most people stumbled over a pronoun for Alex. The reedy voice and the boxer shorts did nothing to clarify. Given her occupation, it was better that she pass as one of the guys.

"Yeah, fine." Bug tapped the blue backpack at his feet and was rewarded with a fist bump from Alex. They'd known each other since middle school.

"It's going great, Scott!" Toby piped up. "Or maybe I should just say "Great Scott!" He chuckled at his own joke, unaware that "Scott" was a nickname earned because Alex was legendary for getting off "Scott free." Ask any runner, and they'll tell you about Los Cerillos. Ten Feds, two runners, a coyote, and one bystander ate it on the Southwest Chief outside of Los Cerillos, New Mexico. Witnesses in the passenger cars reported a lone figure in a skull jacket walking into high desert alone, carrying a duffle bag. Inside were 18 kilos of Bam Bam, cooked in the Tucson Flinstone lab. Alex was the Kaiser Soze of artisanal drug running.

"I'll be in the lounge car," Alex said. "Stay here."

Seasoned runners know the place to be is not the cheap seats. Sure, you have to buy the ticket. But you don't have to sit there. The lounge car is where you want to be. Softer seats, a better view, and instead of broccoli cheese soup smearing through the air vents, you only have the cloudy scent of microwaved hotdogs from the bar below. Trust me in this one thing, the bathrooms on an Amtrak train will kill you. Not the heroin or the hotdogs.

Bug knew the score. But Toby had no idea the danger he was in. Nobody was going to tell him either. We all learn the hard way.

I followed Alex down the aisle. She was no fun on a run. When she was off the clock, she was witty, smart, and we worked on a screenplay, tentatively titled *Riding the Rails*. But right now, nineteen hours away from Vancouver, I could shout at the top of my lungs and she wouldn't turn around to talk to me.

In the lounge car, Alex's mule was waiting. Karen Braunerman, a slender woman in her sixties, a blouse of blue flowers, black capris, and memory-foam flats. For a woman who smelled of Estee Lauder perfume, it seemed an odd choice to be wearing clip-on dreds with blue tips. She'd stuck a Pogues pin on her blouse. Was this her idea of how to fit in with Alex?

"Where'd you go? I missed you." She was breathy with mint lip gloss. Alex sat down next to her.

Karen leaned in for the whisper. "Love you, baby."

Alex nodded.

Karen pulled back, a small crease in her forehead. "That's it, a nod? You love me too, right?"

"I love you as much as anyone loves anyone," Alex said carefully.

Karen appeared to think this statement through, and decided it was a compliment. "Buy me a drink?"

"When we get to Vancouver."

Runners only love you when they're running. But don't expect them to buy you a drink.

"But, baby, I'm thirsty. Buy a girl a gin and tonic?" Cloying treacle. Had this ever worked on anyone? Did Karen even realize Alex was not a man? Despite the I'm-so-in-love tactics, I was quite sure there had been no wiggly-piggly between them. Alex was asexual, among other subtleties.

"Wait. Until. Van. Couver." Alex enunciated each word.

I almost laughed. Almost. I was sure Karen had been given the pre-trip lecture, and just as sure that she'd already forgotten. Namely that having heroin-stuffed condoms in your gut made anything that required a trip to the loo ill-advised.

"Excuse me, I couldn't help but overhear." A man with a buzzed head, Hawaiian shirt, and pressed jeans turned to Karen. "There's a lady in need of a gin n' tonic?"

His smile was easy, another man sat next to him in a similar outfit, their golf bags leaned against the wall. Early thirties, fit, both several drinks in.

Karen blinked and leaned toward them. "Oh, you

better believe it. What are you guys doing here, anyway?"

"Hitting the links."

"I bet you're good at it, big strong guys like you. What's your name, honey?" Karen's come-hither look was even more alarming than her I'm-so-in-love look.

"Zander, ma'am. And you?"

"Cathy," Alex interrupted, just at the same moment that Karen blurted out, "Karen."

"Cathy Karen," Alex said quickly. "Karen is her last name."

"Ms. Karen, huh?" Zander said. "Let me see about that gin n' tonic."

Karen's eyes flicked between Alex and the golfers, calculating. I could almost hear the pennies dropping in the till, one by one. If she thought she was going to make Alex jealous, she was mistaken.

"Be right back." Zander hustled down the narrow stairs to the bar below. The other golfer was suddenly quiet, swigged his drink and dug into a foil packet of salted nuts. Karen looked to Alex for reassurance and found none.

I almost felt bad for Karen. Almost. There was a lot she didn't understand.

She didn't know about Solstice Orion, a doula in Santa Cruz who had Alex's face tattooed on her left breast. Said it hurt like being flayed alive, but it marked their soul bond forever. Karen also didn't know about Otto Mitzel in Seattle, a shy librarian with a dachshund named Tito and a raging heroin addiction. Karen didn't know much about me either, Mina Tanizaki, aspiring filmmaker.

I met Alex at a viewing of *That Obscure Object of Desire*. We both sat all the way through, watching the credits and then noticed we were the only two people left in the theatre. Alex suggested coffee and we talked until 2 a.m. about Bunuel, Cronenberg, and Takashi Miike.

No sex. It wasn't like that. It was worse, really. To love a body is small stakes. To love a mind, in poker terms, means you're all in.

"Here you go!" Zander appeared with a fold-out cardboard food carrier.

"Oh, I could just hug you!" Karen leaped up and did so, lingering a little too long where her cleavage touched his chest.

"You must be desperate," I whispered to Alex. But Alex only rubbed the tiger's eye amulet on her neck. I guessed that was a sign to be quiet. I had no skin in the game, and she knew it. Alex never asked me to carry for her, which is about as sentimental as she got.

"Gin n' tonic are my favorites." Karen sat down. "What's this?"

"Hot dog," Zander said. "Thought you could

use something a little beefier than this, uh, guy?" He gestured to Alex.

The reference to gender sailed over Karen's head and landed on Alex's impassive face.

"Oh, honey." Karen's voice dragged out. "How many calories are in that thing? I only eat once a day. I'm watching my figure."

"Nothing wrong with your figure." Zander smiled wide, and Karen leaned in like a trout with a hook in her lip, downing the gin n' tonic and crunching on the ice cubes like she was 17 on a bar stool in East Philly.

"So what do you do, Cathy Karen?" Zander asked, his beard razored to an inch of its life.

"Me?" Karen splayed her fingers across her chest. "I answer phones for WeLo Construction. You know that run-off trench by Highway 1? We built that!"

Alex's jaw clenched just the slightest, and she rubbed her ear lobe. That was her tell. I followed her gaze behind me, where it landed on a young guy entering the lounge car. A tall Asian man in a hoodie, sweats, and sneakers. Nondescript except he had long pinkie nails and Gucci sunglasses.

He walked by the pitch-black observation windows slowly, as if enjoying the view. The golfers didn't notice him. And Karen didn't either. Just Alex's hand slowly sliding down to the pocket of her jacket and waiting there.

It was a curious thing that Ming Li, son of Dragon

Li, should show up on the same train as us. Despite the triad tattoo on his neck, Ming was educated at Yale, and had settled into a luxury condo in Vancouver. His father owned three jets and a mega yacht. Ming wasn't exactly the type for public transportation. He looked over his shoulder briefly at Alex, then continued walking, out through the doors that divided the cars.

"Think I'll stretch my legs," Alex said.

"What?" Karen's lips donut'ed in disappointment, like she expected Alex to hang on every word she was telling the golfers about the provenance of pot holes. Zander's smile started to crack, like even he couldn't pretend this was interesting.

Alex followed after Ming. I did the same.

They stopped in the metal-lined anteroom by the doors of the next car.

"Who's the chick?" Ming asked. "Karen from secretarial?"

The corner of Alex's mouth twitched. "Actually, she *is* named Karen."

"What's her damage, hanging all over those Feds?"

"That's her problem, not mine."

"She talks?"

"She doesn't know enough to talk. What is it you want, Ming?"

Ming let the pink duffel bag in his hand drop to the floor by Alex's feet. Some blond robot in a school-girl uniform.

"Wow. High fashion," Alex said.

"Don't laugh at Sailor Moon. She's rich, that girl," Ming said.

"Yeah, but she's high maintenance. What're her terms?"

"Leave the X-Lab shit where it belongs, in the toilet. Take Sailor here, walk out rich. You work for us now."

"Um, yeah, about that. X-lab will kill you, kill me, kill everyone on this train, if I show up in Vancouver empty-handed."

"X-lab is dead."

"First I heard of it."

"This morning. The whole place torched."

Alex's face remained placid. "That would make the last merch of X-lab worth a lot."

Ming shook his head. "Sailor Moon is the future." Ming tapped the bag with his foot.

"Let me talk with my friends," Alex said.

"Friends?" Ming smirked.

"Let me talk with my friend-like associates."

Ming shook his head. "Think fast, man. Next stop is Shasta. That's where the Feds bust." He took something out of his pocket and threw it down by the bag, making a wet smacking noise as it hit the metal floor. Toby's loop-de-loop moustache quivered, still attached to the gummy edges of his lip. It didn't seem likely that the face it had recently belonged to was still alive.

"You really do have bad taste in accessories." Alex

reached the tip of her boot out and slid the severed 'stache into the corner, a smear of something viscous following it.

"I'll take Sailor off your hands." Alex picked up the bag. "Bug with the blue backpack is in coach. Keep Moustache Boy as a bonus. Dig deep; he'll pay off."

"And the secretary?"

"Wait until Shasta. She goes to use the toilet, do what you will."

Ming Li nodded and left through the coach seats. Alex slowly moved her hand out of her pocket. The breath she'd been holding escaped. The indifference she'd been sporting dissolved. I moved close to her, put my mouth near her ear.

"What are you doing?" I kept my voice soft. "You're going to drop Bug? He's your friend."

Alex was quiet. I moved closer, lay my cheek against her neck, wrapped my arms around her torso, tried to will some light into her, some softness. All I felt was emptiness, the echo of unanswered questions. She'd been colder since Los Cerillos, harder to reach.

She put her fingers around the tiger-eye amulet. "Sorry, Mina," she said under her breath. "I had to do it." Alex unzipped the Sailor Moon backpack just enough to ascertain she was carrying upward of a million, then quickly zipped it up again.

I watched her posture straighten, the cool calculation making a mask of her face as she walked back to the lounge car.

"Asbestos isn't so bad." Karen was on her second drink and had moved to sit closer to Zander. "It gets a bad rap, you know? I breathed it in for years, and nothing wrong with me, right?"

As soon as she saw Alex, Karen darted up, flustered. A burble came from her stomach, loud enough that everyone in the lounge car heard it.

"I need to use the restroom," Karen said, her hand sliding over her stomach. "I shouldn't have eaten that hot dog."

"Wait until Shasta," Alex said, her mouth tightening.

"Wait until Shasta?" Karen's voice ascended to a mild shriek. "Scotty, I have to go potty!"

"What, Karen isn't allowed to go *potty, Scotty*?" Zander laughed. "I'll take you to the restroom, young lady." He stood up, all six foot five of him.

Karen looked at Alex with supreme satisfaction that said, *See, he knows how to treat a lady!*

Alex shrugged, although a tinge of red crept at the edges of her hairline, maybe thinking about the mess this would make with Ming Li, or maybe the half kilo of pharmaceuticals that was packed in Karen's two lower orifices. Intestinal distress and heroin don't mix well, especially when Uncle Sam's crooked cousin is walking you to the crapper.

The remaining Fed stared at Alex now with undisguised enmity.

Alex scribbled on an Amtrak napkin and handed it to him.

I could guess what she'd written. Something like "Ming Li on the train. Dragon Triad. Check the bathrooms for bodies."

I imagined Toby's lipless corpse tucked like a well-groomed, odor-free carry-on, between the toilet and the wall. His last earthly memory would've been stink. So much stink in the world, and Toby would never get to battle it. Somewhere in Borneo, the Sun Bears were having a jamboree.

Compared to Ming Li, Alex was small fish. The Fed crumpled the napkin and walked quickly out of the car, to the bottom level.

Alex exhaled, pinched the bridge of her nose. "Think," she muttered.

I put my palm on her arm, moved close again. "The luggage car. The windows. Remember Chico?"

Alex nodded, as if she'd come to some conclusion.

The train halted in Shasta as the sun cracked the tips of the pines. Through the track-side window, I saw the Feds take Bug away in handcuffs, Ming too. Alex shoved a screwdriver in the top of the window of the luggage car and jimmied it down. I stood behind her, straining to hear anyone coming toward the door. For six feet tall,

Alex was nimble and fast. She slipped out the half-open window, landing on the side of the train that faced away from the station and the flashing lights.

Then it was just a hop over the gravel by the rails, and she was into the trees, carrying a Sailor Moon duffel over her shoulder, and a black backpack from the luggage car. Bug's blue backpack was filled with Pearl Jam cassettes, a decoy. Bug would do a few years for the heroin bagged in his ass, and then he'd be out. But Alex's black backpack that didn't look like anything to anybody? Enough X-Lab salt to start a seven-nation army. Alex walked into the trees, Scott free, and I followed after.

The local cops would find Karen soon enough, a gash on her forehead where she "fell" so hard against the sink it broke the skull. They'd make forensics search for any merchandise in her orifices, but they wouldn't find anything, unless they looked in Zander's golf bag. There they'd find shit-stained condoms full of heroin. But what cop ever asks to search a Fed's bag?

Collateral damage isn't anything to them. Otto Mitzel, librarian, found bloody in a bathroom on the Texas Eagle. Solstice Orion, head left in the sink on the Empire Builder, body's whereabouts unknown. Mina Tanizaki, on the Southwest Chief, shot in the forehead by a Juarez coyote who thought she was a runner. That was a year ago. My body was dumped somewhere near Los Cerillos from the moving train. When Alex figured out what had happened, she jumped off and walked back to find me. I watched from above as she crouched over my body. A single fat drop of saltwater dropped from a cynical blue eye, landing on my cheek.

"I told you, it's dangerous." Alex had taken the tiger's eye amulet from my neck and put it on her own. I've been with her ever since, her trailing conscience, whispers curling in the shell of her ear.

I guess you could say I love her. As much as anyone ever really loves anyone else.

Spiders from Mars

2170 WAS NOWHERE. 1970, that was where it was at. Tommy Stardust was born two-hundred years too late. Stretched out in his wrinkled, white satin trousers, tucked into starry platform boots, floating off the cusp of Earth's outer orbit, Tommy manned the cockpit of what Stevie called the biggest heap of metal in the galaxy.

"Why don't you get a new rig?" Stevie always pestered him, said she wouldn't overnight with him until he got a better ship. Truth was, he liked it this way, alone with his old things. Some people wouldn't know a priceless antique if it was sitting on them. Tommy gazed out at the firmament through the mottled cockpit. The stars understood him. The vast silence, the spaces between civilizations, that was the place he belonged.

His eye caught on a slight rustle under the pizza box he'd had z-linked for dinner.

"Sentient pizza," he mused, and thought that might make a good title for his second novel; if he ever wrote it. "Yeah, Sentient Pizza...augh!" His hand smacked down on the emerging spider before he could even identify what it was. Now it was a black pulp with yellow innards oozing out on his dashboard. *Spiders in space.* Was that even possible? Maybe it had come in with the pizza.

"Heh." He smiled. "Maybe it's from Mars." He reached up to his carefully ordered ingots of data, more than 100,000 songs from the only decade in the only millennia that mattered. "B...B...Bowie, yeah, that's the one." He slipped the right ingot out and made to insert it in his pristine replica 2130 player. But he missed and accidentally activated his com link, which had been flashing for the better part of a month.

"Tommy?" Stevie's face appeared on the screen. "Thank God you picked up. There are some guys here. Something about a bordello in Colony 9 and an unpaid bill. I told them, you're not that kind of guy."

"Good thinking." A flush of remembered pleasure rippled through his body. Colony 9 bordellos, now that's where a man really lived. *Green tits and purple love kits,* that was the tag line of Martian Kink, his favorite bar. His tab there was substantial. But he always paid, eventually. Brock Fez, bouncer and part-time exotic dancer, should know that. "Tell Brock I always pay," he said before he remembered who was on the other end of the line.

"You mean..." Stevie's voice faltered. "You actually went there?"

"Research, honey." He coughed. "For my novel."

"Oh." She blinked. "Okay."

"You settle up for me," he said.

"I can't." She looked miserable now. "I don't have any money."

"What does that mean?"

"I spent my last three paychecks on your silver boots. You said you needed them."

"For the album cover." He nodded. "My expenses are extensive. You said you were all in, Stevie. *All* in."

"Yeah, but I don't get paid until next week."

"I think it's time to consider..." he let the words hang, ominous, "an open relationship."

"What? No, I won't—"

"An open relationship with your *current job*." He hit the ball home. "You need to work for other people. More than one person. Play the field. See if Vanya will give you some shifts at the cryo-plant."

Stevie was quiet for a few beats.

"You know I'm taking you with me, when I hit it out of the galaxy with this album."

She nodded.

"Extra shift," he said with subtle tenderness before switching off the com.

Stevie was a slender slip of a woman with angelic eyes, blond hair so big it rivaled the supreme being's, but her voice...Tommy could not string together words to encapsulate the sounds she made on stage. Except that Typhoid Goat Debacle would not be an undue name for her first record. She had the funny idea she was the reincarnation of a singer from that most holy of decades, and Tommy was too polite to tell her that if reincarnation or time travel were possible, he'd already be on stage, he'd be a rock god. Still, in her fawn-colored platform boots and white lace, Stevie caught as many looks as he did. It was a shame about her ports. But he was a gentleman. When he made it big, he'd buy her new ones, glow-in-the-dark sparkle ports.

The call with Stevie had him stressed. Tommy's groove was ruined; he might as well get it over with. He pressed play on his messages. Thirteen from creditors. *Delete*. Two from fans. Those were worth following up on. He was polite and punctual with fans. Three from Spacelink, informing him that his card had hit its limit and did he have any way to pay for his intended three-month rotation around Earth? Something about being towed out of orbit if he failed to pay. Another about being shot of out orbit if he didn't pay immediately. He skipped those. One message from Racine, then another, "Where are my chapters?" *yadda yadda*, "Where are my goddamn chapters you fucking whore," *yadda yadda*. She really needed to relax. He wasn't even working on his novel. No. First, his debut album. Once that launched, all his financial problems would dissolve. This work was so radical, so pure, so historical it was *futuristic*.

"I need to relax, man." He flipped gravity off, let it all float. He drifted out of the captain's chair, up into the cabin. The pizza box, the Bowie ingot, the spider carcass, everything floating around him. His hookah, perhaps his best friend in the universe, floated by, and Tommy partook. Smoke was technically a fatal liability in most space ships, but his ship was used to it. Tommy exhaled, and watched the smoke twirl in chaotic, weightless ribbons. There was no "up" in space. The smoke wrapped around him. For a minute, he thought he saw smoke outside the cockpit window, a thin veil of it, a scarf of white drifting across the glass. Then the quick flash of a face, dark eyes looking at him. It reminded him of someone, but the name slipped his mind. A spider floated past him, all eight legs wiggling. A string of silver woven in its wake, landed on him and stuck.

Tommy took another inhale of the hookah, and let his mind slip, let his consciousness drift out of his ship, into the quasars and black holes and dark matter of space. He was everywhere. He understood everything. If only he could weave it together, drop it onto the page as words. Maybe Racine would get off his case then.

"Major Tom?" the ship inquired.

"Ground control?" Tommy wasn't sure how long he'd been out. A few hours? Months? What was time to the intergalactic mind? His hands were covered in silver threads, his legs too.

"Your editor is attempting to board."

"Racine? No! Totally no. She *cannot* come in."

He clicked his wristband and the monitor flickered to life. Racine's face was pressed against the space-lock porthole, looking like she'd take a lemon up the pipe.

"I see you, Stardust. Open the lock."

"Can't do it, babe."

"Why not?"

"I'm..." Tommy did a few flips in slow motion. "Molting."

"You punk-ass little bitch," Racine hissed. "I need a chapter, five pages, something, anything. Or Radioactive Press walks."

"I'm working on my album."

"You have a book contract that is a *year* overdue. And you're fucking around with your guitar up here?"

"I'm a knight in white satin," he mused aloud. His Strat floated by. Not a bad idea. He reached for it, and strapped it on. "You can't think in mundane terms, Racine."

"Spacelink called my office. They say you can't remain in orbit without replenishing your card."

"Put it on my tab."

"You don't have a tab."

"Racine, Racine, they've got you clapping for fish like a trained seal down there. Listen to this." He unleashed his Strat space haze on her, the cosmic droppings of his mind. From the look on her face, she wasn't feeling it. He turned the volume up a few notches. He snuck a look at her. But she was almost cross-eyed, staring at something in front of her on the glass.

"How the fuck did you get spiders in your ship?"

"They came with the pizza. Second one today."

"Those are poisonous, you moron."

Tommy sighed. Racine wasn't going to go away easily.

"Ground Control, deliver first five pages of untitled second novel to editor."

He watched as five replica sheets of yellow A4 paper slid through the door trap. She grabbed them like she was going to mangle and bruise them from pure hysteria. Her eyes scanned quickly, her fingers relaxed. Finally she shook her head, as if bewildered that someone like him could write something beautiful. "You talented, talented son-of-a-bitch," she muttered. "Finish it, will you?"

"No problem. Next week, tops."

Tommy watched Racine's mini-pod spark to life and shoot back to Earth. If only he could finish the novel. But the truth was, he'd written those five pages over a year ago, and not a single word since had landed right, just spluttered like ink wreckage on pages that defined detritus. Deep down, he feared the music was just procrastination. Arachne...he suddenly felt a need to speak to her. Maybe, after all this time, she might forgive him.

Tommy scrolled until he found her data and clicked on. Three humming beeps. Then another three. Her com was implanted in her neck, there was no way she didn't know he was calling. Unless reception in the Left Lands had failed. Why she lived there, in fields of radioactive wheat, was her own mystery. She travelled with the Stratos Spectacle, an alien circus, and he'd been hired as an oddity for a while, as "the man from 1970." They'd grown to be friends of an unlikely nature, given that she was a foot taller than him and didn't believe in anything out of wedlock. The key word in Tommy's mind being *lock*. After his first novel came out, he quit the Spectacle, but visited her regularly. She said she was a radical, a revolutionary carrying her freak flag high, and someday the world would change, and what was high would be brought down low. But as far as Tommy could tell, all she did was train spiders for a living, as part of her circus act. She said they were smart.

"Uh, really?" He'd looked at a glass container teaming with eight-legged black death.

"Yes. They tell stories."

"I don't hear anything."

"With their webs. How do you think you wrote your first novel?"

"With a pen and paper?"

She'd shaken her head at him as if she thought he was slow-witted.

"Wait, you think the spiders wrote it for me?"

"I *know* they did. I asked them to help you. How else could a guy like you write an existential masterpiece about love and heartbreak?"

"Huh?" Is that what she thought his book was about? Sure his main character was bummed, but it wasn't over a girl. It was his missing guitar pedal, the Six-Thousand Unicorn bi-pro.

"The problem, Tommy, is that any story, every story comes with a price."

As far as he could see, the price was listening to people's theories about his book. If she didn't have a mighty love for glitter panties and circus chic, he'd have written her off as a lunatic. But the woman had ports that sparkled like Polaris, and she could wear a ringmaster's hat like nobody's business. She too belonged in another time, another place, said she wouldn't sleep with him until she was in love with him. And he'd waited around a long time, at least a week, hoping that might happen. They'd been anachronisms together, until...what? He tried to remember. *Must've gotten bored,* he thought, unable to think of what it was that had driven him to tell her about Stevie. And the bordellos on Colony 9.

He didn't like to remember the way her face fell and her pupils slivered to diamonds, as if she'd known all along that he would disappoint her.

Somewhere between his explanation of male testicular function and the hero's journey and the fine, fine drag of Brian Eno on *For Your Pleasure,* she'd hit him over the head with a mason jar of spiders. He woke up in his ship with a gumball swelling on the top of his skull.

He'd done what any reasonable glam god would do. He booked it for space and stayed there, sulking the better part of a year, using up the last of his savings. Let Arachne miss him a little. He couldn't afford her as an enemy. He'd had baffling moments of truthfulness with her, and she had a damnably keen memory. He considered the worrying possibility that she might contact Stevie and let all the cats out of the bag...and there were quite a few cats. Dana. Raven. Brock Fez at

Martian Kink, who liked to cage dance in white go-go boots and a pink thong, his heavily carpeted thighs frizzing against each other. When he got going fast enough, little sparks of static snapped in the air. But nobody on Earth knew about that, unless Arachne had been running her mouth.

A spider floated in front of him. Then another. Something tickled his face. Silk threads landing there. He realized the cockpit was filling with them, a silvered web. The Bowie ingot was caught in one line. Even his hookah was no longer free-floating. Along those lines of silver, little black bumps reflected the light of the cockpit on their inky carapaces.

"Hey, what are you guys doing?" He went to lift his hand up and found that he could not. But Tommy wasn't one to panic. "Is this how we're going to write the second book?" He wondered if Arachne hadn't been right after all.

"Ground control," he croaked.

"Yes, Major Tom?"

"Com Stevie Nicks."

"What do you want?" A gruff male voice came over the speakers.

"Who is this?" Tommy demanded. "Where's Stevie?"

"She can't come to the phone. She's working her shift."

"At the cryo-plant?" But the roar of hooting behind

the man's voice suggested this was not the cryo-plant. "Brock?"

"Yeah."

"It's, uh, you know, it's—"

"Stardust. I know who you are. Little guy with ports the size of Saturn's rings. Lousy tipper."

Tommy sputtered. It didn't matter which port Brock was referring to, either would be an insult. "I mean, wait, Stevie is working a shift and you have her phone?"

"She's working off your bill, Stardust. Three shifts a night."

"But Stevie can't dance."

"She dances better than she sings. At the rate she's getting tipped, she'll be here a while."

"You bastard!" The roar of lions came from his chest. "I will bring the fury down on you, man, like, like...the fury!"

"I already had it, remember? Okay, not much to remember." Brock laughed. "You want to be the man about this, why don't you dance off your own bill? I got a thong from when I was five that might fit you."

"Garrrrrr!" The molten lava welled up in his throat, followed by complete helplessness.

"Yeah, that's what I thought. Say, how's the novel coming?" There was laughter, and then the com blanked out.

"Ground control!" Tommy shouted.

"Yes, Major Tom?"

"Do something!"

A few seconds later, his second favorite song of all time piped through the cabin. Something about loneliness and not being the man they'd all hoped.

"I'm a rocket man," he whispered, watching a constellation of shapes appear in the spider web in front of him.

"Com my editor," he croaked.

He expected Racine to pick up. But he didn't expect her face on the screen, eyes lined with red.

"Hey, Tommy." She was walking through the city, hunched at the shoulders.

He couldn't, at that moment, remember exactly why he'd called. "Racine, where do you think stories come from?"

"If I knew that..." her voice trailed off, as if her meaning was obvious. It wasn't.

"Do you think there's any way that spiders could, uh, write a story in my mind and me not notice?"

Her eyes settled dead on the center of the screen. "I told you those spiders are poisonous. You're probably going into toxic shock. Ask your ship to administer venom antidote."

It came back to him what he was calling for. "I need help, Racine."

"That's clear." Normally this was the point in the

119

call she started swearing at him.

"Stevie got into some trouble, and I need an advance."

Racine didn't say anything.

"I'll have the book to you next week. You can count on that."

She paused in walking and looked up, as if asking for forbearance.

"Okay," he said. "I shouldn't have called you a clapping seal. But Radioactive Press can—"

"They fired me." Her voice broke. "I showed them the first five pages. My boss has had it. I've been selling him on your second novel for three years. Five pages just wasn't enough."

"But—"

"I'm sorry. I believed in your book, I really did. I believed in you." She looked like she was crying now, that kind of silent, sneaky crying that somehow was more deadly than operatic fireworks. "I can't help you. You're on your own, Stardust."

"What does that mean?"

The com went dead. The spiders were massing around him, thousands of eyes in the cockpit, silvered and unblinking.

"Ground control. Exterminate spiders."

"Cannot exterminate spiders without exterminating all life forms. Proceed, Major Tom?"

"No!" Tommy shouted. "Turn on gravity."

The ship turned on gravity, but Tommy didn't drop. He hung suspended in spider silk, like some kind of a fly for a feast.

"Not cool, man. I'll write the stupid novel. Is that what you want?"

But the spiders didn't speak, just knit their wicked little legs at top speed, and Tommy started to see images in the webbing. Stevie, staring at him. Racine too. Dana, then Raven. A field of faces, then Arachne last of all. Their expressions somber. Tommy started to feel a little, hunted.

The women, woven in spider silk, didn't speak, but from the corner of their eyes, diamonds sparkled, then dropped in slow motion, attached by spider thread. They looked like tears, he thought, or stars sparking in the dark reaches of space.

Tommy felt something foreign. An ache in his throat that cracked into his chest, a heaviness in his eyes, something more desolate than the space between galaxies, something lonelier than his chosen exile. They'd loved him, these women, their regard like quasar trails, following him through space, no matter how far he travelled. Arachne's face loomed larger now, her eyes crystalline and black. Her face pale and translucent, she moved toward him.

"We gave you the story, Tommy. We gave you everything." Her mouth was near his now, red and beckoning. Tommy's mouth hung open in befuddlement, and found she was kissing him, softly, an enticement of roses that caused his entire body to tense. A simple kiss that would lead to simple mechanics taking over. Except Tommy opened his eyes and thought he must be seeing double, then triple. Not two eyes on Arachne, multiple eyes, almond and bulbous, black satin with a shine that reflected world within world. Eight of them, dancing in front of him, mouth stretching into a smile. Sharp teeth.

"Every story has a price, Tommy."

"I—" He opened his mouth to defend himself, and found her mouth on his, the softness of roses turning to something viscous, a moistness there that repulsed him. His mind bled out the back of his skull. He saw himself suspended, covered not by Arachne, but a large spider, her mouth depositing something into his mouth. Eggs. He shivered, disembodied and helpless, his thoughts going numb. He saw further afield, to Colony 9, Stevie hoping he'd save her. He saw Racine in the city, out of a job, staring up at space, wondering why she'd bet her career on him. And more pressingly, he saw the cruiser hovering outside his ship, apparently serious in their threat to blast his ship out of orbit. But there was nothing he could do now. Tommy Stardust was just a thought, just a song, a forgotten string of words, floating in space. His boots sparkled, and David Bowie played as the final kiss occurred, the final story never to be told.

★ ★ ★

On Earth, the bone brittle wheat in the Left Lands clacked like porcupine quills against each other. Arachne walked through the radioactive field, her spider-web stockings catching the light of sunset. She'd been looking up at the dusk-soft sky for some time. Until she saw the blip of shiny metal plummeting toward her, the periphery in blazes, a plume of black smoke behind it. Tommy Stardust hitting mortal velocity. Burning, burning. It gave her no joy. She'd loved him more than he would ever understand. But like all men, he gave up easily. And his death was a necessity. Her spiders were flameproof. And they knew the way home, even if Tommy Stardust didn't.

A jarring boom as his ship hit the ground, pregnant with a new species of arachnid, something larger and deadlier than most humans could withstand. The freaks would rule. She'd make sure of it.

The Closet

A SHORT, BALD MAN in a wool coat and coke-bottle glasses: Edgar Pierpont was no oddity on the corner of Broadway and Wall Street. Except that it was 70 degrees in mid-May and his bulky coat went from his throat down to his ankles.

I crossed Broadway, my teeth brightened and blond highlights refreshed a week ago, when I received a hand-written note:

Ms. Balducci,

I wish to engage you in a property search. All particulars are negligible, save this: a spacious closet in the Southeast corner of a building built before 1895 of four or more stories, on the top floor. It must have walls of 12 feet, generous lighting, and no crawlspace above.

I will meet you in a week's time on the corner of Wall Street and Broadway at 10 a.m. Look for a white carnation in my coat lapel.

-E. Pierpont.

Greg, my boss, had shrugged when I showed it to him. "Rich weirdo. Pierpont wants a closet, give him a closet for the gods."

"No phone number, no email...this is mob stuff." I shook my head. "He doesn't say a price range or a neighborhood, how many bedrooms, nothing."

"Antonella, guys like that don't give price ranges. Show him the penthouse on 5th. Have you Googled him?"

"Yeah. A recluse, he runs the Pierpont Institute, no photos online. Who has no photos online?"

"They pay people to scrub that stuff from the Internet. Trust me, this guy is rolling large. You need the money, right?"

That had stung. Yes, I needed the money. Badly. Tim had left finance, left me, and taken half our assets to Uzbekistan to rescue street mutts. The twins were a year away from college. I'd stopped waiting in vain for alimony checks and gotten my cert in real estate.

"Ms. Balducci, I expect punctuality, I certainly do," Mr. Pierpont, so noted for the white carnation in his lapel, said with no preamble. My outstretched hand froze in awkward solitude. I checked my phone. It was only 10:02.

"I apologize, Mr. Pierpont," I said hastily. He was my height, not a big man, save for the bulbous stomach that protruded under his coat.

"Well." He looked at me through his shaded glasses, a size too small for his round face. "I assume you have assembled a list of acceptable properties."

"Yes, of course." I flashed him my whitened smile. "The first is on 5th Avenue. 5.5 mil. Let me get a cab."

"I assumed you would have a vehicle of your own. A real estate agent with no vehicle of her own, or a vehicle she does not feel confident in showing a client. I'll wager you barely earn 60,000 a year. Perhaps I made a mistake in contacting you."

My pride spit back. "70K, Mr. Pierpont."

He pursed his lips, then muttered, "Very well."

I hailed a cab and then watched him wedge himself in, that voluminous stomach like some kind of flotation device. All attempts at small talk failed. I resigned myself to silence, until we arrived at the green awning over the door to 965 5th Avenue.

My heart-rate sped up as we ascended to the twelfth floor, the park spread out under our view. My cut of 5.5 mill could put Angelina and Melania through M.I.T, better than old mom had ever done at Hackensack

Community College. We were moving up. I could taste it.

The private elevator opened into opulence. Fully staged with modern furniture, windows ten feet tall. I waved my hands large, rattling off the features I'd memorized. A ten-person sauna, a La Cornue stove, temperature-sensitive windows that shaded in sunlight.

He exhaled heavily, like a bull impatient to charge.

"Ms. Balducci, these details do not interest me in the least. Take me to the closet. The one that you will surely have ascertained faces southeast."

"Okay, fine." I led him to the master bedroom. He marched into a closet that was bigger than most Manhattan walk-ups.

I imagined myself in a new Gucci dress, the proud mom, front and center, having her photo taken with her upwardly mobile daughters in graduate gowns.

Mr. Pierpont looked at the closet walls, snapped a small metal contraption out of his pocket, something that looked like a sphere of interlacing gold rings with an arrow in the middle.

"This is unacceptable." He shoved the device back in his pocket. "I specifically asked for a closet in the Southeast corner."

"But it is—"

"It is two degrees off, Ms. Balducci. *Two* degrees off. Precision is utmost in all matters of stellar alignment."

"Stellar alignment? Mr. Pierpont, Manhattan is a grid. I can't make them move the city."

"I made a mistake with you, Ms. Balducci. Good day." He thumped on stubby legs back to the elevator.

"Mr. Pierpont, wait." I ran after him and squeezed in before the elevator doors closed. "Give me another chance!"

He stared in the opposite direction, making me wait. "I will need to make some calculations of my own before we proceed."

"Yes, okay." I exhaled. "What can I tell you?"

He took out a small notebook and flicked it open. His pen was a Montblanc with a sapphire embedded in the cap.

"Now then. Your date, time, and location of birth."

"What?"

"I wish to ascertain your sun sign and rising sign, Ms. Balducci. It will tell me if we are compatible in this venture."

"I don't know the time. I was born on January 5th, 19...82."

"Do not prevaricate, Ms. Balducci. You are clearly in your—"

"Fine, 1972."

"The time. I cannot make my calculations without precise data. Maiden name."

"Balducci *is* my maiden name."

"That will have to do. A Capricorn." He shook his head. "You don't have the determination of a Capricorn. Let us hope your chart has other compensations for what I suspect is a lazy mind, prompted into a new career past mid-life, out of desperation. I'll wager there is an ex-hustand currently squiring a young girlfriend around Long Island in a red Corvette."

"Schnauzers," I said. "He's saving Uzbekistanian schnauzers."

Mr. Pierpont paused. "The BARK mission in Uzbekistan? Run by Mr. Silverlake?"

I nodded.

"I fund them a great deal of money. Mr. Silverlake, I assume that is your ex-husband, is a Taurus with an Aries moon. A dependable man. That is why I funded him."

"Well, he was dependable until he wasn't."

"That is true of most men, I suppose. It's far more sensible, in my estimation, to purchase intimate company, and leave propagation of the species to the Midwest. I seem to recall that Mr. Silverlake mentioned daughters. Two point five, I assume. Jennifer and Alison, no doubt."

I wanted to smack those bread-dough cheeks with an open palm, shiv him in that fat stomach with a newspaper folded to a point, just like they do in Riker's. "Angelina and Melania. And you've never had to work a day in your life, Mr. Pierpont, so—"

"That is where you are so wrong. I will make my astrological calculations and inform you if I wish to proceed. You may expect a message via carrier pigeon."

I stopped in the middle of the foyer. "Carrier pigeon?"

"Yes." He raised his notebook, Montblanc poised. "What is the address to which I shall send the pigeon?"

☆⚹☆

"Hi, Janice." My voice struggled to sound genuine. "How are the kids? And George?"

"Who is this?"

"Antonella Balducci."

"Oh, Antonella. Your number didn't show up on my phone. It just says unknown."

She was shading me. Janice Niak was my doppelganger. We'd started at the same time, had the same waist size, the same mane of dyed blond hair and amber eyes, both from parts of New Jersey that regularly made national most-violent lists. People often confused us at realtor mixers. Well, they mistook me for her. Because everyone knew about Janice Niak who sold Manhattan deluxe, and nobody knew about Antonella Balducci, who sold condos on Staten Island.

"You need a favor, I assume," Janice said.

I grit my teeth. "Your listing. The Ansonia, top floor. I have an interested party."

"I see." Her tone shifted the slightest. "It's 10.6.

Your client can pay?"

I smirked at my phone. "Edgar Pierpont. The philanthropist."

There was silence and I imagined her fuming with jealousy.

"Don't waste your time on Pierpont. I spent three months running around showing him places and he found something wrong with every one. The closet, right?"

"Mmm," I said noncommittally.

"I fired him as a client. I don't have time for that. But maybe you do."

I thought of the sapphire in his Montblanc. "No skin off your nose if I show him the place."

"It's half," she said coldly.

Shit. Half the realtor fee.

"Sure," I said sweetly.

After she hung up, I tapped my pen on my desk. It was odd that he'd gone to Janice and then to me.

I dialed a number with about 10 digits in it, my ear met with Tim's voice, distant, garbled.

"Nella? It's not Monday. Are the girls okay?"

I scowled. "Yeah, the girls are fine. Do you think you can spare 5 minutes for the woman you married?"

The line gargled and crackled. "What is—" His voice cut out.

"Edgar Pierpont," I raised my voice. "He sponsors

your dog thing. I need to know about him."

"Pier..." My ex's voice broke up. "*Something something* dog."

"Does he pay you promptly? Can I trust him? Is he crazy?" I shouted, hoping that would somehow vault the words to Tashkent. But all I heard was "*Something something* good guy *something something* dog."

"Mom, there's a thing in the front yard."

"Well, go get it." I didn't look up from my coffee.

"Mom!"

"I'm trying to meditate, Angelina."

"Drinking coffee is a meditation? That's stupid."

"Go do your homework." I stared out the window. But there it was. Not a pigeon. A gray drone in the middle of the lawn. I ran out and grabbed it. Taped to it was a little orange beak made out of construction paper, and googly eyes next to that. What kind of billionaire painted a drone to look like a pigeon? Attached to one of the "legs" was a rolled paper, as if it really were a pigeon-carrier message.

"Ms. Balducci, Your Virgo rising gives me a small ray of hope that you have the mental capacity to complete your assignment. I will meet you this afternoon at 2 p.m. at the same location as before. I expect you will take my requirements seriously, this time."

I stumbled back when the "pigeon" suddenly came to life and buzzed upward. How long a range did these things have? Was he standing a few blocks away? He could've easily sent me a letter, an email, a text. What billionaire did that? Left the city to spy on his realtor? He'd send a lackey, wouldn't he?

I jogged after the pigeon. It cut across the Morgans' yard. I ran ahead to the cross street. Somehow, I knew, if I caught Pierpont with the drone, he was a fake.

I rounded the corner and saw the pigeon land ahead of me by a grey escalade.

A figure leaned over to grab the pigeon. Without my contact lenses in, I couldn't make out details. But I caught the red blur of a dress. A blond head of hair. I stopped, out of breath, gasping, as the woman slammed the door and sped away.

Maybe Mr. Pierpont was for real. Just weird enough to send a blonde in a red dress to spy on me. I hustled back to my house and shot up the stairs, past the twins bickering about who got to wear the Justin Bieber t-shirt today.

I flung open my closet and ran my hands over the options, paused on my red dress. Something occurred to me. I took out the red dress and held it up in the mirror, my blond hair voluminous and messed. I could send Pierpont a message that said, *I'm on the ball, buddy. I got your number.*

☆★☆

"This is not your car, Miss Balducci."

"What makes you say that, Mr. Pierpont?" I navigated the grey escalade so far up 1st Avenue, we were in danger of rubbing elbows with the Bronx.

"There is a rental agreement in the glove compartment."

I looked over. Had he searched the glove compartment when I got out in Astoria Park to pick up keys? What else had he looked through? I glanced in the rear view and checked that my purse was sitting upright in the back seat, unrifled.

He was once again dressed in his camel coat, although his stomach appeared to have grown. This time it was 80 degrees out. Our fourth place of the afternoon, and he would not take his coat off, not even when the doorman at the Ansonia had offered to hold it for him. The Ansonia was built in 1899 not 1895. It wouldn't do. The studio in Hell's Kitchen had ceilings that were 11 feet high not 12. And not a hint of a reaction to my red dress.

"It would've been nice if you'd told me," I said glumly.

"It was self evident," he insisted.

"No." I squeezed the wheel and imagined it was his neck. "Why didn't you tell me, the 13th?" The moldering shoebox in Harlem had the southeast closet, 12 foot walls, everything he demanded. Except the seller's agent said June for escrow. That's when Mr. Pierpont had insisted, "It must be next week. By the thirteenth. I need to have the key in my hand by the thirteenth."

"I have grave doubts about your mental capacities, Ms. Balducci. The stars are a map. It is a fool who does not consult them. The thirteenth is the quincunx of Saturn and the Comet Belvedere, an event not witnessed since 1895."

"And? You have to have a closet facing southeast? You have enough money to buy God. Why not just build your own penthouse in the right place, with the right closet?"

"Small minds, Ms. Balducci, small minds."

"Let me drive you home, Mr. Pierpont." *Drive you out to the Pine Barrens, club you with a crowbar, leave you dead and rotting...*

He looked at me through round lenses fogging with disdain. "Your driving is atrocious, Ms. Balducci. Twice you have offended the traffic laws of New York. I will certainly not have you drive me to my abode. You may take me to Wall Street, as usual, and I will disembark there."

"Fine." I proceeded to the financial district and brought the car to a halt, cars honking behind me.

"If I may say..." He looked at me critically as he stepped out of the Escalade. "Red is not your color.

136

Good day."

I thought about it, revving the engine and plastering his fat little carcass all over Wall Street. He looked back at me from the sidewalk and squinted. He was waiting for me to leave before he walked anywhere.

Where are you going, you little shit? I glared back at him.

A cop tapped on my window, forcing me to advance forward. But I waited at the end of the block, craning back to see him descending the stairs to the subway.

"I'd like to speak with Antonella Balducci, please."

"Yeah, that's me." I struggled upright in the recliner, a bankrupt bottle of chardonnay lolling in the shag carpet by my feet, CSI muted on the TV in front of me.

"Ms. Balducci. This is Jennifer Goodman at First National."

"Okay." I woke up more fully. "What can I do for you?"

"There was a problem with your payment to Washington Mutual."

"What?" That was my mortgage payment. I was really awake now.

"There are insufficient funds in your account to cover the payment."

"There's upward of 400 grand in my account."

"Our records indicate you withdrew that amount yesterday at 3:34 p.m. from our Flushing branch."

Never cross a Jersey girl. I drove my minivan right onto her yard, crushed the mailbox, and slammed into her perfectly manicured hedge of roses.

A few seconds later, the front door flew open, and George Niak came flying out the door. "What happened? Are you okay?" he asked as I opened the car door. Quick on his heels was Janice, in her robe.

"You." I pointed my frosty pink nail at her, and took the baseball bat with me. "Thief!"

"What the hell is wrong with you?" She frowned.

The security video had been plain as day. A woman of my height, my hair, even wearing identical Prada heels to mine, had walked into the Flushing branch at 3:34 p.m., presented my driver's license, my password, all of the personal information needed to convince the teller she was Antonella Balducci, and then to close out her account. There was only one woman in town who could pass for me, who would do something that vindictive and low.

"You think I stole your money? That client in East Orange was mine. Don't go delusional on me now."

"Not East Orange," I growled. "My bank account. Yesterday at 3:34 p.m. in Flushing."

"I was in Secaucus yesterday, closing a deal on a three-story castle. If you got robbed, that's your problem. Call the police. And get off my lawn." She held up a baseball bat of her own, while her husband, lily-livered piece of shit that he was, dialed the cops.

☆⚡☆

"Yes."

"Yes?" My voice went hoarse. "You're sure."

"Yes. This is will be adequate," Mr. Pierpont said of the run-down one-bedroom in Harlem, four stories above a liquor store and a massage parlor. A cockroach skittled across the floor by his Bruno Magli loafers. He had a red moustache on his face that hadn't been there a day ago.

"Excuse me a minute." He entered the bathroom with the broken toilet, and closed the door after him.

I heard grunting sounds, huffing. What was he doing in there? Something obscene? When he opened the door, I half expected him to have his junk in his hands. Instead my eyes glued to a stack of green. His moustache was hanging off one side. His coat was still on, but his stomach had shrunk. And he looked to have at least 300 grand in his thick little fingers.

He walked closer to me, and my hands automatically reached for the money. He retracted, a smirk creeping on his face. "No, no, that wouldn't be wise, would it? You may call the seller's realtor now and ask them to come here. 350k, cash."

★✸☆

"This is your fault, Tim!" My voice assaulted the phone as I floored it over the East River, the twins crying in the back seat.

"What are you talking about?" The connection, for once, was clear.

"I'm losing the house. And that woman, that whore, stole it from me."

"Who stole the house? I don't understand."

"Janice Niak went to the bank, impersonated me, took the entire account. How am I going to pay the mortgage?"

"Did the police arrest her?"

"They think it's me, they think I robbed my own bank account. But it was Niak, I know it. She had enough time to drive to Flushing on her lunchbreak." That had been crystal clear when Janice showed up to the Harlem one-bedroom in record time. She'd informed Mr. Pierpont of my recently suspended realtor's license. Mr. Pierpont said he didn't care which realtor acted on his behalf. So I was out, and there was Janice Niak bagging the realtor fee for one trip out to Harlem. And all those weeks I spent working for Mr. Pierpont were down the drain. Not to mention my life savings stuffed somewhere under

140

the mattress in Janice's house.

"And another thing," I shouted at Tim. "Why didn't you tell me about Edgar Pierpont? You said he was a good man."

"Mr. Pierpont? He is. Funny you should mention him again. He's been here this week. Got right in there with the crew, shoveling the kennels, putting out food. A real hands-on kind of guy. Never expected a billionaire to like dogs so much. But you know, you can tell a person's soul by whether or not they like dogs."

"Fuck you." My voice started to fade from yelling. "The Chihuahua was an accident, Tim, *an accident.* I'm supposed to guess, no sign in the rear cameras, he's peeing behind my wheel?"

"You never liked Mr. Buns," Tim said tersely. "Not one tear you shed. Not one. You never liked dogs."

"You never liked our daughters," I shot back.

"They're princesses. You turned them into monsters."

"Dad," they objected in unison from the back seat. "We can totally hear you."

"Good job, *Dad*," I declared. "You finally admit it. Don't like your own daughters."

"I don't even know them," he objected. "You had them off at cheerleading camp and swim practice. I saw them an hour a day, max."

"Well, guess what, buddy, now is your chance to get to know them."

"Oh my god, what have you done?"

"What am I about to do?" I swerved onto the off-ramp toward LaGuardia. "I'm putting them on a plane to Tashkent."

"No," he said weakly. "This is a third-world country, you can't send the kids here."

"It's that or my Aunt Michaelina in East Orange. You tell me which is worse."

It was only after I hung up and ejected the girls out of the minivan at LaGuardia, that it occurred to me. If Edgar Pierpont was shoveling dog shit in Uzbekistan last week. Then who was the weirdo I'd been showing apartments to?

"We get that a lot." The perfectly coiffed woman at the large mahogany desk on the first floor of the Pierpont Institute nodded.

"Who is he?" I tapped my nail on the desk like a dagger.

The lady shrugged. "A man in Mr. Pierpont's position attracts many odd characters."

"So what's this guy's scam?"

"It's not really a scam. Javier Consuelo. Upstate New York. He changed his legal name to Edgar Pierpont. He is, as far as the police and our private detectives are concerned, a citizen searching for an apartment. There is no crime in that. It came to our attention a year ago, but as no laws were broken, there was nothing to do."

"And the bullshit with the astrology stuff?"

"The Mr. Pierpont you inquire about is an astrologer. He runs a legitimate online business, Starsigns."

"You're shitting me."

"I suggest you go to the police, if you can prove you've been misused."

"How about this?" I stood. "You pay me ten grand to walk out of here and not shoot my mouth off to daytime TV about fraud involving Mr. Edgar Pierpont the billionaire."

"Ms. Balducci." She smiled, as if her day was brightening. "That is extortion. And our conversation is being recorded." She pointed up to the corner of the room, where a little eyeball was installed. "I understand you already have an outstanding case against you for assault. Kindly leave."

Javier Consuelo AKA Edgar Pierpont sat in the middle of the closet in his white boxer shorts with red hearts on them, a coat hanger bent into the shape of a pyramid on his head, his arms wrapped around his knees, tight black socks cutting off the circulation in his pasty calves, which were oddly hairless. His whole body was.

"Mr. Pierpont?" I looked down on him with concern.

143

"I mean, Javier. What are you doing?"

He giggled. And rocked back and forth, his eyes like a boiled frog's, gelatinous and moist.

Next to him on the floor was a Styrofoam cooler and a roll of toilet paper. A biological funk hung in the air. Next to that, restaurant packets of saltines, the kind that come with a cup of soup. An unopened can of diet coke. That would explain the crust of saliva dried at the corner of his mouth. Above him on the closet bar, his camel coat hung. No other clothes. It suddenly occurred to me, he might've been wearing nothing underneath it, and that's why he kept it buttoned up to his neck. The Bruno Magli loafers were there. But something peaked out behind that coat. I moved it on the rack. A red dress. And behind the cooler, a size 10 pair of Prada heels, a blond wig, and a bag of cosmetics.

The "woman" operating the drone. The "woman" emptying my bank account. Javier Consuelo, in drag? I thought back to everything I'd said to him that first day. Everything he'd teased out of me. That I make 70k, my birthdate, my address, maiden name, the names of my daughters. It wouldn't take him long to guess my password for everyting was *Angelina*. My purse left alone with him in the car. Had he photographed my driver's license, my social security card, while I ran around town trying to find a closet that faced southeast?

I grabbed the wallet sitting on the cooler and flipped

it open. Card upon card embossed with my name.

"You picked me because we're the same height," I said.

"And a Capricorn," he said. "Stubborn, a thick skull. With a low voice."

"Low voice, are you kidding me? I'm a woman! You picked Janice Niak because she's the same size too..."

"A Virgo. Too hard to fool. But she proved useful in the end."

"You stole my life savings to buy this shit hole? So you could sit in the closet in your underwear?" My voice ascended to glass-cutting sharpness. "And shit in a box with a coat hanger on your head?"

"They're coming." He rocked himself even harder. "Soon. So soon." Beads of sweat ran off his forehead.

I belatedly noticed that he had a small revolver tucked in one of those tight socks.

"Put my wallet down and leave, Ms. Balducci. It will all be over soon, hmm, yes, soon."

I slammed the closet door shut and dragged a kitchen chair in front of it, levered it to keep the door closed. He was trapped in there. With all the evidence. Now I just had to get a police officer to take me seriously.

My report of a cross-dressing con-man half naked in his closet with a pistol in his sock did not fall on sympathetic ears.

"Lady, maybe you're telling the truth," one cop had said. "But there are some things I don't wanna see, know what I mean?"

It takes a con artist to beat a con artist. I contacted my cousin Vince, who I hadn't talked to in ten years.

"That's easy. You make up one of those whaddyamacallits, make him sign a thing, sayin' the apartment is yours. Then you sell the apartment. Get your cash back no problem."

"He has a gun."

"A big one?"

"No."

"You're in luck. I know a guy."

A day later, I entered the apartment with a juicer from Camden known as the Muffuletta.

"In there." I pointed at the closet, which still had the door jammed shut with the chair. Javier Consuelo hadn't been out of that closet, I knew that much.

"Stand back." Muffuletta rammed the closet door with the bulk of his body. There was no explaining to a guy like this that the door opened outward. Finally, winded, he kicked the chair out from under the doorknob.

The door swung open, creaking as it did so, half hanging off the frame. I waited for something, a gunshot, yelling, something. But Muffuletta just shrugged, looked at me over his shoulder, and then wandered off to the kitchen, to see if there was anything to eat.

The closet. I approached gingerly, with disbelief. It was empty. Not just empty of "Mr. Pierpont." But the cooler, the toilet paper, the wool coat, the saltines. Even the wig and Prada heels were gone.

It wasn't just Mr. Pierpont who had vanished, it was my 300 grand and any hope I had of regaining my good name, my realtor's certification, or my life.

On the floor of the closet, where he'd been sitting, the wood was scorched in a circle. I looked up. Same on the ceiling. A black stain of soot there.

"Nothin' to eat." The Muffuletta wandered back in the room and looked in the closet again. "What, this guy set himself on fire, or something?"

"He couldn't have. There would be bones, a smell, the rest of the closet would've gone up too. All his things are gone."

"Crawl space up there?"

I imagined Pierpont in his boxers, leaping up and down to reach the trap door. Even if he'd somehow balanced on the cooler full of refuse, and managed to leap up that high, catch the door and somehow lift himself up...well, he wouldn't have done it in drag, and he would've had to somehow lift the cooler up there with him. There would be something left in the closet. "He's too short." I shook my head.

"Maybe aliens abducted him." Muffuletta laughed.

Maybe Pierpont had been right about the quincunx of whatever. What did I know? My house was being repo-ed, and Janice Niak was pressing charges for an alleged swing I took at her with a baseball bat. My career as a realtor was done. The twins were probably earning a living the hard way in Tashkent.

"Where to next, boss?"

I only had one place left to go. "East orange."

"Whatcha gonna do there?" Muffuletta asked.

"Stay with my Aunt Michaelina. Maybe go into business as an astrologer."

"You believe in that weirdo shit?"

"No. But it pays big, Muff, it pays big."

Mt. Auburn: Danse Macabre

LAFAYETTE HAD EXPECTED to spend the night in a Harvard dorm room or a basement in rent-controlled Chinatown, not a crumbling Victorian in South Boston. Ringed by weeds and dirty needles, the house was a mauve mourning gown, slowly slouching into the uneven sidewalk. The woman next to him on the bed was no less macabre or inert, unaware of the danger she was in.

"Oh, dark goddess." The lump of fishnet and doom groaned. "Make it stop."

"I can't stop the sun from shining." Lafayette didn't like the light streaming through the curtains any more than she did. Strange symbols swam on the slate-grey ceiling of what had once been a fine parlor, now stripped down by the years. Lafayette knew the feeling. Rendered in chalk were drawings of Hecate, a murder of crows, the scimitar moon. Sigils of sorts. Signs. Every Goth girl in Boston had one tattooed on her arm.

"Coffee. Coffeeeeeeeeee. Must—have—it." The pile of regret moaned, face down on the bed. She likely thought it was cute to moan and speak of thirst. Twenty-somethings thought everything they did was cute. She knew nothing of thirst. *Nothing.*

"I am not kidding. Coffee." A thin wrist extended itself and waved a knife with a crescent moon on the handle. New Age stores carried them in bulk now, ceremonial athames. Her blade was silver and a good instinct on her part, although he doubted she knew how to use it.

"Amusing athame," he said. "It's your house. Are you really out of coffee?"

She lurched up, hair ravaged by the coital ritual that had left Lafayette largely unruffled. But through her black strands of hair gleamed a neck that made his jaw click. A paining streak of hunger blew through him.

She looked at him slyly. "You haven't eaten or drunk anything since I met you last night."

"Call me a picky eater." He wondered if she was truly young. Perhaps the night had played a trick on him. A chance meeting, it had seemed. Walking through the grounds of the Evensong Mansion, lit with Jack-o'-

lanterns; couples had promenaded in swaths of plum, violet, and black. Most had been graduate students and club kids, thinking it would be an adventure to go farther than the Red Line's last stop. But she had seemed different. Too still. Leaning against an elm tree in devastating black silk. He'd asked for her company, offered his arm. Walking through the ghosts of hydrangeas and roses already succumbed to fall's first frost, he'd felt the intriguing sensation of belonging. It had led him back here, to her house.

"Are you straight?" she asked with no warning.

"Excuse me?" Lafayette turned his full attention to her.

"You didn't seem that interested in me. It's okay if you like guys. Just say so."

Lafayette hid his surprise. Most women were too mesmerized by his presence to notice his lack of engagement.

"Interested in you, yes. In the act? No. I derive no pleasure from such things, Moon Dark." He used her Goth moniker. Her real name was probably something intolerable like Patty or Karen. He produced his phone to mollify her. "Three shots?"

She brightened. "Pumpkin spice frapp."

"I didn't take you for a pumpkin spice sort of woman."

She looked at him reproachfully. "Get a pumpkin seed muffin for Mina too."

"Mina?"

She smiled at him, and for a moment it seemed there was something sharp in her eyes. He should've fed last night, when she was floating in a cloud of pheromones. He'd done it often enough, met plenty of girls at Goth events, but inevitably beneath their black corsets beat ordinary hearts with ordinary dreams. It made it easier for him that twisted wardrobes so often belonged to the straightest of souls. A quick glance toward Moon Dark's open closet suggested that for her, jeans and sneakers would be a costume.

Lafayette scanned his phone until he found a café with the necessary muffin and beverage. The irony was upon him as he pressed purchase. Nothing for him.

Moon Dark got up from the bed, body round and magnificent with a snake tattooed up her spine, and hair like Medusa's. She paused under a section of the ceiling with broken boards and whistled lightly.

Lafayette wasn't in the habit of breathing. But he stopped all pretense of doing so when a full-sized raven hopped down from the gap and landed on the naked woman's outstretched arm. Its dark beak lay flat against her lips, brushed over her face.

"Nice canary," he grumbled.

"Mina destroys what does not deserve the night," she said cryptically. As if it were nothing out of the ordinary, or worse, nothing that she intended to explain to him, she walked into the bathroom with a demon bird perched on her shoulder and closed the door. The hiss of the shower followed.

The hunger was obscene now. This couldn't drag on any longer. A stabbing in his temples, a longing in his veins. He dressed and then paced the boards. On the table in the middle of the room lay a spread of tarot cards, crystals lined around them like a demi-stadium of spectators. Over it, a ring light and a camera, a list of appointments. Something must drive a woman, young or otherwise, to rent a derelict parlor, make a meager living by the cards, and yet spend her money on things like the Evensong Ball. Perhaps one night was not enough to discover what that was. Then again, some enigmas were better buried.

He walked quietly to the bathroom and opened the door just a crack. It would be the work of a moment to surprise her with a kiss on that expanse of soft flesh, to watch the delight in those hazel eyes, and then their dimming.

But the raven was there. Observing him. Claws like switchblades. There was no mistaking it for a crow. It perched on top of the shower rod that surrounded the clawfoot tub. Moon Dark stood under a stream of water, her body a shadow behind the shower curtain.

He calculated. The bird did the same, one eye tracking him.

"Let me guess," he muttered. "Nevermore?" He pivoted away from the bathroom, down the stairs and to the front door. The sound of a vehicle's engine shutting off, the slap of shoes on the sidewalk, then the creak of the porch floor. Cologne lathered like mayonaise on bread. Lafayette didn't prefer men, despite what Moon Dark might think. But he was too famished to dicker about the menu.

Lafayette swung the door open, took the Frappuccino in one hand and the man's neck in the other.

"Hey!" the man objected. Although like most, he found the shock of his neck being crushed and ripped open too much to process or defend against. Lafayette's teeth bore down, gashing the skin. Beautiful warmth gushed into Lafayette's mouth, a rich sustenance that only human blood could give, something of the man's soul in the liquid. Lafayette had tried the blood of deer, of cows, of fish. It only made him ill. This was the necessity of his genus. It must be the blood of man. Or woman. Really, women tasted better, and that was a culinary statement, not a sexual one. It took little time for the man to go limp, crumple down, silent. Lafayette tossed him behind the pile of firewood stacked on the porch and scanned the houses across the street. Not the kind of people to call the police.

The delivery man was something to someone. To Lafayette, he was a latte.

Back inside, Lafayette set the drink on the counter, and tossed the pumpkin-seed muffin toward the gap in the bathroom door. A black beak poked through, stabbed the offering, and dragged it back into its steamy den. Lafayette really should go now. It was unlike him to linger.

"I'm begging you to drag me down with you, to hit the last nail in," the warbling of misquoted lyrics came from the shower. Lafayette shook his head in pained humor. She was a sigil doodler. An off-key Cure fan who kept an athame under her pillow. And a raven in the attic. Perhaps Moon Dark was, at last, the dinner that was too charming to devour.

"I'm going soft," he grumbled and dipped his pinky nail at the corner of his mouth, using it to write in red on the butcher block counter.

Mt. Auburn Cemetery, All Hallows' Eve, midnight *–Lafayette.*

Living in a cemetery was harder than Neville thought it would be. But his subjects were here at Mt. Auburn, Boston's celebrated Victorian cemetery. And he was nothing if not dedicated. His rain slicker lay hidden behind the Isabella Stewart Gardner mausoleum. His bedroll and poncho secreted along lanes with dainty names like

Primrose and Hazel Dell. In the morning, across the way, the Persian bakery left bags of stale za'atar mana'eesh and baklava. Yet his bones ached from sleeping rough, and the groundskeepers were always checking, prying, weeding. But he knew perfectly well how to sit on the bench by Mary Baker Eddy's grave and look like any other rumpled academic.

His worn loafers sank into the wet grass in front of his favorite grave. Rain-slicked leaves the color of rotting banana peels and wrinkled lunch bags massed at the base of the upright marble, one of thousands of genteel headstones tempered by New England's brutal seasons.

He knelt, and the knees of his corduroy pants immediately dampened. The earth here was gloppy under the grass roots, would come up by the handful if he wished, rich with worms. Their worm ancestors had long ago digested Miss Grace Elliott, beloved daughter of a wealthy steel family, consumed by typhoid in 1875. Carved into the stone was *Dance with the cherubim now.*

"Ah, Miss Elliott," he whispered. "I am the only one who remembers you. Without me, you don't exist." Neville pulled out his notebook and a worn pencil. He sketched the stone, the statue of a woman in neo-Roman garb dancing above it. The definition of her hips, breasts, all carved expertly. His research showed the mother, Anne Elliott, had been scandalized by the carving.

"Short-sighted simpletons," he muttered under a

thistly beard. "What is the harm in admiring the female form? If done with respect, with careful consideration." He ran a finger over the contours of the dancing woman.

"Sir, the cemetery will be closing in twenty minutes." A voice startled him.

He twisted around to find Ellen Kincaid. Grave docent and head of the local historical society. She volunteered her time here, leading tours. As if a B.A. from Wellesley gave her any authority to speak on such things.

"I'm almost done with my research," he said.

"You say that every day."

"That is because I work every day. Unlike the fatted cows of Harvard Yard."

"The Yard hasn't kept livestock since the seventeenth century. And Dr. Kellington has already written a peer-reviewed paper on the graves of Mt. Auburn." She nodded toward the gravestone and he realized his hand, in grasping for balance, had landed squarely on the dancer's bosom. He snatched his fingers away. There would be time for that later, when the moon rose and the lovely stone figures of Mt. Auburn belonged to him.

"Yes, well, Dr. Kellington is not the last word on nineteenth-century funereal practice. He does not understand the stones as I do. They hold memory. They are alive." He put his notebook in his pocket and fingered his pencil. It was dull at the point, but not so dull that it couldn't make an impact on skin. His species was, in the end, ridiculously easy to puncture. But not the stones. The stones were forever.

"Gates close in eighteen minutes." She wrapped her maroon cardigan around her spindly torso. Above her the spidery arms of an apple tree, almost black in the gloom.

"The grounds do not close until 6 p.m." he insisted.

"On most days. But not on Halloween."

"I do not see why a vapid holiday should disrupt my research. The gates will stay open until 6." He gripped his pencil more tightly.

"I'm sorry, but I have to lock up early. Too many college kids running around, wanting to get drunk and… well, whatever it is that they like to do." She said it as if she'd been born in support hose and mothballs, had never been young. "And there was that one year…that poor black cat." She leaned in and whispered, "Satanists, you know."

"That was 1991," he snapped. "And likely a fox got to it, that is all. *The Herald* blew the entire thing out of proportion. Now, if you'll excuse me."

But she didn't budge. Perhaps she thought him a frail old man, rumpled and pathetic.

"It's getting cold." Her voice echoed over the stones. "You won't be able to stay here come December. It's too cold. A recipe for hypothermia."

"Your concern is neither welcome nor necessary. I

will be leaving by the West Gate at 5:59, as usual."

"And coming back in via the East Gate while I secure the other one. I've seen you. Since May. Since that thing in the papers. I recognized you from the picture." That would be the picture of him being escorted out of Dudley House in handcuffs. While that smug Kellington watched from his office window.

"Witch hunt," Neville said.

"You taught there for thirty years. You must have a pension. There's no need to stay here like this, wearing the same clothes every day, suffering. I haven't wanted to say anything, but I worry what will become of you in the winter."

He recognized the staunch New England morality that handed out soup and warm gloves in church basements all over Boston. But such mercies meant nothing to him. He was above pensions, four-wall cages, even congestive heart failure. The doctor had said, "Get your affairs in order." But that was three months ago. The stones were all that mattered now. They kept him alive. He turned his back on her and pretended to examine the lichen on the stone, until he saw her grey shoes walk by.

I wonder how much he paid you, that Kellington, to spy on me. He sent you, just like he sent the others.

She paused at the end of the lane. "Professor Freeland, if you won't leave Mt. Auburn peaceably, I'll have to contact Harvard's mental health services. I realize it was a great shock to you, a tenured professor with a book on the Belgin Short List, being discredited for, well, let's call it an indiscretion."

"You can call it whatever you like, Ellen."

She jerked back, as if her name were not written on the bent copper tag on her chest.

He felt his bile rise. "I'd call it the calculated plan of a she-snake to smear my name, sent by none other than the very professor you seem to take as an authority on funerary display. As if he owns these stones."

"She-snake? Really, there's no need to be rude. She was just a girl. An undergraduate."

"It was her mistake. To come with me, alone, out to a deserted graveyard. Nobody to hear her cries."

Ellen's forehead creased like a quilt punctured by a needle. "I'm sorry, what are you saying? The papers reported it was harassment."

"Which one, Ellen? Which girl? So many of them here at Mt. Auburn. *So many*." Neville chuckled. "Living in a cemetery is harder than you might think. But dying in a cemetery is easy."

Too late, fear lit in Ellen's eyes. She darted over the swell of grass, her form dwarfed by naked oak and elm. Far off, the wrought iron gates of Mt. Auburn. Between here and there, so many steps.

Neville stood and fingered the blunt pencil, his shoes wet with the pliable dirt at Grace Elliott's grave.

★✦★

Even on Halloween, Moon Dark was a spectacle. She supposed taking a raven on public transportation justified the stares. But she refused to get in a cab. Boston drivers were lunatics.

"What is that?" Frankenstein laughed, hanging onto the handrail as the train lurched toward the next station.

"Corvus corax," Moon Dark said, Mina perched on her wrist.

Frankenstein, evidently a few beers in, reached his mitt forward, like he wanted to pet Mina.

Moon Dark pushed past him, ignoring the stares from pregnant nuns, dead cheerleaders, and escaped convicts on the Red Line. She sat, replete in latex leggings, black glitter boots giving her an extra half foot, a brocade long-coat of black dahlias down to the ground. And a silver chain from Mina's foot to Moon Dark's wrist that was strictly ornamental. Mina perched on her leg, still as a statue, murderous eyes tracking Frankenstein.

"Not yet," Moon Dark whispered. "There is another."

She rode to Harvard Square and strode through a throng of undergraduates in plastic masks, all of them certain of becoming very drunk and hopeful of becoming very laid. Frantic music poured out of bars, so far removed in time and place from the crackle of the fire and the lone fiddle that had been Moon Dark's first soundtrack. Up

Mt. Auburn Street she went, Jack-o'-lanterns winking on porches. She remembered well enough when it had meant something, the candle in the darkness, a demon's face carved to scare away evil things. Some of those evil things still existed. Lafayette was such a thing, she supposed. But the means to ward them off were mostly forgotten.

The street darkened into the suburbs, until the brick wall of the cemetery appeared, behind it miles of disintegrated bones. She paused at the iron fence of skewers that looked like medieval spires.

"You're needed," she said to Mina. The raven cawed three times and the gate creaked open, the lock undone. She slipped in. Away from the last of evening traffic, into the snapping twigs and owl calls of the dark cemetery. There was no wind, but a current was at her finger tips, stirring her ebony locks. Her eyes sharpening, something of the crescent moon in them, her birthright.

Mina seemed agitated, eyes darting.

"What do you see?" Moon Dark ran her fingers over Mina's feathers, and waited until the images came to her. Somewhere in this place, a shambly man hunched over a grave, stroking it, talking to it. A disturbing display from a broken mind. Moon Dark's stomach turned. Mina's claws flexed.

"Later," she said. "Find the other one first." Moon Dark unlatched the bracelet around her raven's leg. Mina flew ahead, and she followed, until she saw the silhouette of a man leaning against a tree. He came into view, a figure who seemed unhurried, indeed, likely had nothing else to occupy himself. Just as he had seemed at the Evensong Mansion, although then, she'd hoped there was chivalry beneath the pale skin and velvet.

"Good evening, Moon Dark. You look lovely." His charm, like some kind of fog, crept toward her, wanted to wrap around her.

Guillotines hung from her ears. A metal choker circled her neck. A wiser man might've read her mood. But Lafayette seemed happy to see her.

Her eyes narrowed. "You called my athame amusing."

"Perhaps it is."

Moon Dark's blood pressure, already at a simmer, began to boil. "And you called my familiar a canary."

Mina flapped her wings in the tree, the branches rustling.

"You're a cad, Lafayette. 'I take no pleasure in the act'? Needless, ugly words. You're the worst kind of cad."

"Calling a vampire a cad is a gamble on oblivion, Patty."

"Calling a witch 'Patty' is certainty of oblivion, LeStat."

His face grew even paler, a spark of true anger in his eyes. Well, at least he'd read a book in the last century.

"A witch? Let me guess, online 6-week course. You're a priestess of the Fruit Bats of Isis."

163

"Why invite me here, if you thought I was mundane?"

"A late-night snack. Why did you come, if you thought I was a regrettable lover?"

Moon Dark's palms shook with welling anger, glowed a violent blue, something she could not hold back any longer.

"You left a dead man on my porch." She let fly a deluge of hellfire, a hex on her lips rewarded with a guttural shriek from under the tree and the smell of burnt velvet.

She waited, scanning for any movement.

"Now that was rude, Miss Dark." His voice startled her, right by her ear, and then the sound of his cursing after he bit down on her silver choker and was retarded by the metal.

"Break a fang?" She watched in satisfaction as Mina banked down suddenly and dragged a claw over his neck, a thin thread of red appearing there. He clutched his throat in patent disbelief.

"You have no idea what kind of bargain I had to strike with the criminals next door to get rid of that damn corpse!" She threw her hands forward, another burst of blue fire, another shriek from Lafayette. "And his stupid car!"

Then there was silence. And she thought he must be gone. Mina flew back to her shoulder and perched, the raven's cool beak against her flaming cheek. "Well, he deserved it, didn't he? Just a serial killer in the end."

A bemused laugh, quiet and marred by a cough came from the graves a few steps away. Her anger spent, she had to admit, it was a relief to hear his voice.

"If I'm a serial killer, I'm not the only one in this cemetery." His face came into focus, scorched up one side.

"That man." Moon Dark nodded. "Mina doesn't like him."

"Neither do I. If I thought he had a tolerable flavor, I'd rid the world of him."

"You tried to bite my neck just now."

"In my defense, you did cast fire on me." The smile he wore was the first genuine thing she'd seen from him. He reached into his pocket.

A little blue flame of warning lit at her palms.

"It's nothing like that," he said. Instead he produced something wrapped in brown paper. "Has Mina ever tried a kouign-amann?"

"Are you trying to bribe my raven?" Moon Dark bit her lip as Mina launched into the air and plucked the pastry from his hand.

"Nobody can resist these. Well, among the living, anyway. I cannot enjoy the taste any longer. But in Brittany, I recall the wonders of butter and flour magicked into something that made life seem worth living."

Mina settled on a branch and let out a series of happy pips as she savaged the pastry.

"Are you serious?" Moon Dark whisper-hissed at her familiar. "You like him now? One pastry and your mind clouds?"

Lafayette laughed. "My hearing hasn't suffered with the centuries. Perhaps I should've brought a Frappuccino for you, Moon Dark."

She colored. Pumpkin spice was her weakness.

When did you know I was a vampire?" he asked.

"When I met you."

"I see." He blinked and limped closer. "Yet you invited me to your home."

She didn't like to admit it. But it was there, of course it was. "I hoped you'd be good company." She'd meant it when she kissed him, when she let him gather her, widow's silk falling to the sheets. She did not invite men home out of habit, went for years without thinking of such things.

"I *can* be good company. At least I was, some years ago. Perhaps of late, I'm less so." He advanced closer, ash grey eyes aglow. He was, she admitted, beautiful. That was part of why she'd accepted his arm. The other part, she didn't want to say. He guessed anyway.

"It's lonely," he said. "Isn't it?"

She looked at the ground. Then nodded in accession.

"There are fewer of us, these days," he said. "Many of your kind burned. Most of my kind have destroyed themselves rather than go on. To feed on the species you once belonged to...I suppose you think me beyond hope."

"I didn't say that." Moon Dark raised her chin. "I thought you unfeeling. And a cad. As if it's been far too long since someone called you to account."

"It's been far too long since anyone has seen me for what I am..."

"And still cared for you?"

He nodded. "I wonder if the same is true of you?"

She shrugged. "People make assumptions. And they really shouldn't. I do no harm. Unless..."

"Yes?"

"Unless someone really cheeses me off."

"It seems I am the cheese. Let me introduce myself. I was born Mathias de Lafayette, in 1782. And I've not had company I valued since 1810, when my wife died. I must feed to live, if this may be called living. And to feed, I choose to give something in return. An evening unlike any other. I find dinner less painful that way. You are the first to notice my distance, and I apologize that I hurt you. Also, about the body on your porch..."

"Oh, that." She stared at him pointedly.

"I occasionally become, what is the word they use now? Hangry."

Her lip tickled, but she refused to give in to a grin. It would be smarter to turn on her heel and go home with Mina, spend All Hallows' Eve as she normally did, alone. Let another decade slip by before she gathered enough hope in humanity to hunt for company.

Mina pipped.

"It's a bad idea," Moon Dark muttered to her bird. "He'll just disappoint us."

"I believe I already did that." Lafayette cocked his head. "I'll endeavor not to do so a second time."

Moon Dark frowned at him. He raised his eyebrows, humor dancing there.

She sighed and extended her hand. "Abigail Good, 1692, Salem Village."

"Abigail." He bowed. "It's All Hallows. Almost midnight. The veil thins, and many of our friends, long gone, are due. Will you join me for a danse macabre?"

By a cold Hunter's moon Neville's eyes devoured the graves, more frankly carnal than he dared to be during the day. He scrambled up the angel statuary, his hands trailing the voluptuous figure of "My beloved departed Maria," his lips passing over the stone mouth, his hand cupping her breasts. Then he leaped down, crept up on the curvaceous grave of Patience Lester, his fingers tender and so gentle. He tamped the grass down with his feet where she lay.

"They really ought to check these things, once in a while." He smiled to himself, then continued his rounds.

All night he would do this, trancelike, until he fell down from fatigue, slept feverishly, dreamed of them even then.

"Good evening," he said over the newly disturbed earth at Grace Elliott's grave.

As if in answer, the chords of a fiddle, like a cry, arrested Neville. It was nearby, a high-pitched wail of mourning, and then the plucking of strings suggestive of composition, of movement. He froze as he heard something from Grace Elliot's grave. A sigh. As if the music called to the stone. As if the stone itself listened and longed to respond.

"I knew it," he said. For so long he had posited that human memory lived within the stones, in the figures. The academy had denounced him for it. But he was not imagining this. A hand emerged from the stone, made of moonlight. He could see the trees through it, knew it held no dimension, and yet...he reached forward. The lady's spectral fingers scattered like smoke at his touch.

"No, no," he stepped back. "We must be respectful."

She emerged from the gravestone as if it were a door, her figure phosphorescent in a fine ball gown.

Grace Elliot, 1875, she whispered, and then walked past him, somnambulistic in her drifting steps.

Neville's spine was gripped with chills as he saw wisps of light rise from the other graves. Illuminated, the boundaries of the figures blurred into comet trails as they moved, then caught up to them, rebounding into the shape of literary Victorians in white gowns. *Louise Chandler Moulton, 1908. Amy Lowell, 1925.* Each whispered her name, the date of her death. Yet even those who had died old, looked as fresh as lilies upon a grave.

"I know you," he said, spittle gummy at the corner of his mouth.

But they did not stop for him, did not see him. They moved toward the music, a Bohemian waltz. He followed, his heart beating shallow and fast, the possibility upon him that he was having a psychotic lapse. He raced after them like a small boy trick-or-treating for forbidden sugar.

The chalky specters gathered in a clearing by the mausoleums. In the middle of this, two figures, distinctly corporeal, danced. Although from the glow of their eyes and the dance of spirits they seemed to have séanced into being, Neville had to conclude they were not human. The man appeared antiquated with burn marks on his face, the woman wore Gothic clothing. Jet black and glitter. The plucking of delicate strings by unseen hands, perhaps a cimbalom, the swift base of a cello, and the humor of an oboe, added to their swaying.

The beautiful, lovely things Neville had spent months sketching began to dance, circling the couple in the center, who moved a little faster now, the woman's black coat spinning out behind her, lifting. He saw in their regard for each other something foreign to him, or at least forgotten, some sentiment he'd felt when he was young, something as simple as a blush of color to the cheeks, as complex as a novel being written between two pairs of eyes. He'd shut it off in his teens, that troublesome red juggernaut that interfered with clear vision and dignity. But perhaps here, his work come to life, he could allow it to beat quickly, to feel.

Neville stumbled as he jogged around the ghostly circle, twirling, falling down, then doing it again. Wisps of their beings brushed against him like lace. Joy surged through him. Lighter than air were his feet as he lept. He flapped his arms, hummed the tune aloud, and waved his hands like a conductor.

"Am I dead?" He pinched his arm. But no, he felt that. "Still alive!" he declared, spinning, around and around, between the silken specters, their whispers dizzying him. *Elizabetta Moseur, 1895. Letitia Gold, 1901.* Their names wreathed him, the ultimate memorial. He had become his work, had at last found the truth of death, of memory.

The pale man in the middle of the circle laughed at something the woman said, exposing needle-sharp teeth. And when the man gestured, ghostly Jack-o'-lanterns appeared in the air, circling around the dancers. The woman who danced with him seemed lit from within by her own smile; she blocked out the moon with it as she watched the pumpkins with the glee of a young girl.

We are all children in the end, Neville thought, *in the face of death.*

Summer Johnson, 2019, came a whisper, and Neville stopped his dancing and craned his eyes. His head whipped around, scanning the trees and hedges.

She stood, watching him. No dress. No sachet of roses at her wrist. Just a jeans skirt, Keds, and breasts pressed against a soft t-shirt. Summer Johnson smiled at him, and Neville's sweat gelled.

Ellen Kincaid, today. A reedy voice slapped his ear and he cowered low to the ground, all of his manic exuberance severed. Ellen stood over him now, just as pinch-mouthed and dour as she had been earlier in the day. Summer Johnson joined her. And then, *Jenny Sharp, 2019,* in a sundress and straw hat, also staring at him. All of them the shadows of skeletons that rested over ancient coffins. He'd laid their bodies fresh over women who had died a hundred years ago. Nobody knew his victims lay there. Nobody had thought to check.

"You can't touch me," Neville said. "Go back to your plots. Nobody else knows where you lie. Only I do. Only I can remember you properly. Without me, you cease to exist."

Ellen Kincaid leaned over him, voice calm and cool. *To live in a cemetery is hard.*

The other two added, *To die in a cemetery is easy.*

And then, their final pronouncement voiced in three,

You do not deserve the night.

Neville saw something in the air, gliding, something black, a bird with a wingspan of four feet or more. It came at him, slashing his soft neck, the carotid expertly flayed down to his vertebrae, severing his spinal column. He lay there, helpless, warm liquid erupting from his veins. Above him, Ellen Kincaid, Summer Johnson, and Jenny Sharp watched, impassive, waiting, as if they knew, when his soul was ripped from his form, it would be theirs.

All around them, the ghosts of Mt. Auburn danced, skirts billowing, rising into the air, driven by a waltz that spiraled ever faster. The two figures in the middle took flight in their upward spiral, the bright stars of All Hallows' Eve blinking like fire flies above them. Neville's blood fell into the thirsty ground, the earth seeming to suck at him, draw him down, into the worms, into the dark nothing, unnamed and unremembered.

The Fortune Teller

THE SILVER GHOST threaded through the skyway like a silk scarf, pearlescent vapor trails streaming past. At the top of the world, Noveau Deco angels stood on gold buildings, pronouncing man's triumph over the collapse of nature. No other traffic marred the skyway; a buy-in of 350 Hex assured that Fairfield Hughes's vintage Silver Ghost had a lane to itself, three miles up from the surface. Above him the dusky, muted dome of heaven gave way to purple, then black, stars closer to him than any other man on the planet, still bright, still available to wish on. Were he in the habit of wishing.

Fairfield twisted his head to be sure he wasn't followed, suspicious of every lit window. Every corner could be an ambush. Even at this height, political assassinations were possible. Fairfield ought to know.

He'd paid for enough of them to occur.

"Turn down, here," Fairfield said to his chauffeur. The ground level was the last place a man of his stature belonged. But Fairfield was running scared. The military police couldn't guarantee his safety. He needed to see her.

Tercer glanced at him in the rear-view mirror. "What's our destination, Sir?"

"Never mind about that." Fairfield buckled his jump belt across his chest in preparation for descent. He liked to keep his plans secret from everyone. That's why Stilton, his synthetic man of affairs, didn't ride in the body of the craft with him. Even before the Helio Exchange had informed Fairfield about the short, he'd been secretive. A smart habit for a wealthy man. "Turn down. Now."

Tercer turned the Silver Ghost, long nose pointing to ground.

"At this hour, calculated course is drastic, Sir."

"You're under full warrantee. Show some nerve." Fairfield regretted his words, as he recalled that Tercer was programmed to fly 9-8 fighters, and had done so in the last two victory campaigns.

Fairfield bit his tongue and shrieked as Tercer dropped the Silver Ghost, plummeting. The exquisitely timed descent shot them through traffic on lower airways with inches to spare. The craft shook as they pierced the cloud belt, so that Fairfield's sensitive stomach ballooned up in his throat. As they blasted downward, his eyes rolled back, an incoherent "cheeee-yah" burbled on his porcelain white teeth. When they emerged, it was to a world cast in darkness, save for the gargantuan floodlights. Toxic rain fell without relent, glittering in the columns of blue light. If the Silver Ghost wasn't coated with Arnium 5Z, it would be corroding like all the junkers on this level.

"Our final destination, Sir?" Tercer inquired, the craft paused.

"The Dragon Room. A-132.98."

"Sir? The Dragon Room is not—"

"Do it." Fairfield heated at the cheeks. He knew it wasn't advised. He knew it was a gamble. But he needed to see the Fortune Teller.

The Silver Ghost descended further, then stopped like a coin snapped to a magnet, hovering a foot above the ground. Fairfield, breathing heavy through his nostrils, smoothed the flaps of his red hair, wiped the bile from his moustache, and ran his pinkies over his eyebrows. His first wife, the only real woman of his experience, had called him vain. His fourth wife thought him cold-hearted, and that was coming from a synthetic pleasure model. His tenth wife, injected with circuity that obliged her to flatter him, was the keeper.

Dreary earth-bounds in protective coats darted by

on acid-eaten walkways. Fairfield lowered his window just the slightest, and his nostrils quivered. Stench. They said disease ran rampant down here. As if to prove it, a shambling, drunken man veered toward the craft and slapped it hard, laughing. Fairfield shrieked and jerked back. His security cubes sprang to life, floating above him, driving the drunk away with high-voltage prods. A flutter of health sensors crowded Fairfield, scanning.

You're uninjured, they said with his mother's voice signature. *Take care, Mr. Hughes.*

Fairfield straightened his white bow tie. There was no putting it off. His first time to touch his foot to ground level. He swung the door open and stepped out into air, forgetting the gel buffer raised the craft up by a foot. He fell into an inky gutter of oil and mud and excrement. Fairfield shot up, his sensors clamoring around him. *Exposure to bactolycilin,* one said. *Applying antidote.*

Several security cubes hovered around him.

"Stilton," Fairfield barked. "Now."

Strapped to the back of the craft by the spare turbo, Stilton unbuckled his jump harness. Fairfield found it pleasing that Stilton bore an uncanny resemblance to him.

"Announce us, Stilton."

"Of course, Mr. Hughes, certainly." Stilton held an umbrella over Fairfield as they walked toward the marquis, a trail of security cubes and health sensors in a merry-go-round above Fairfield's head. A racy jazz chorus caused the glass windows to vibrate and quiver, as if ticklish.

Stilton stepped up to the ticket window. "Mr. Smith is here for his appointment."

A wiry man in a stained tropical shirt looked up, his hair in long blond tubes, his teeth in neon caps. Some kind of street decoration, Fairfield surmised.

"No synths allowed," the man said. "You go in, you go in solo, Mr., uh, Smith."

"No, I'm sorry, that's not acceptable." Stilton pressed his nose to the glass. "Mr. Smith is an important man and he cannot, he will not proceed without his retinue."

"Then Mr. Smith can piss off. No synths in Dancer's place." The guy went back to reading some form of news printed on paper. The headline was "Hughes Manufacturing Charged with Manslaughter: Has Fairfield Hughes' luck run out?"

Stilton went red in the cheeks. "I don't understand. Arrangements were made with a Mr. Lyle."

"I'm Lyle."

"Then you know we're here to see—"

"Dancer's lady, yeah. If Mr. Smith wants to see her, he's going in solo. House rules."

"Well, I certainly take offense, sir, I certainly do. I am not synthetic. I am not," Stilton said.

The man held up a scanning device that looked a

few decades behind the times. He shook it a few times until it beeped. "My mistake. You can go in. And your boss. But the tech entourage stays out here."

It was dumb luck they couldn't tell Stilton was a newer model, a hybrid synth imbued with human genes. It was better Fairfield didn't go into the Dragon Room alone, although he wasn't as defenseless as he seemed. Fairfield adjusted his shirt sleeve to cover the gold cuff on his wrist and swept into the Dragon Room without his security cubes or health sensors.

Real women scared Fairfield. And the Dragon Room was full of them. Chorus girls in short bobs and tight curls, brassieres made of zirconia, catching the light as they shimmied and threw their legs up in unison, heels clicking on the shiny floor of the club. Despite his wealth, he usually struck out with real women. They said it was his lack of affection, his secretive paranoia. But he knew it was his name that repelled them.

The fast, slick sound of horns had the entire place bobbing and tapping their feet. Dancer's place oozed low-rent glamor. Champagne but not Bollinger, patrons in tuxedos, but not Bergdorf. Cheap knock-offs. But the women weren't. Fairfield could tell by their imperfections. The curl out of place, the chipped tooth, the beads of sweat. He shuddered. They might even have body odor and mood swings and free will. Yet he was having trouble looking away.

The singer, a singular, statuesque woman stood in front of an old-fashioned silver microphone. A periwinkle top hat and platform heels boosted her into the stratosphere, raven hair glinting like polished patent leather, breasts cupped by black satin, a short skirt of chiffon, and then...Fairfield's stomach shrunk in on itself. Double orchid garters down rounded thighs, onto baby-blue stockings. And in the middle of it, the heart of the matter, a glimpse of black satin when she swayed and the skirt floated upward. Fairfield began to sweat. And he did not like to sweat.

"Evening, Mr. Smith." Dancer, an elegant man with a waxed pencil moustache shook Fairfield's hand and led them to a table.

"I'm not sitting here," Fairfield said. "Take me directly to the Fortune Teller."

"Cool your heels." The man laughed. "You don't like my club? It's not bad, as waiting rooms go."

"It's a common ploy. Make me wait, so I'll buy a great deal of champagne first. Never mind with the milking and bilking segment of the evening. I don't have time for it." Fairfield tossed several par-Hex at Dancer, who caught them like a professional ball player, although his bearing was more of the ballet. Maybe he really was a dancer.

"Sure. You wait in a private room, then." Dancer gestured for him to follow.

"I thought so." Fairfield walked past prying eyes that looked him over, perhaps recognized him. He felt naked without security, only Stilton tripping behind him, lip hanging open at the variety of females here. What kind of short-circuit in a synth allowed for lust? Must be the human genome. Fairfield didn't like it. Stilton was destined for deactivation.

"Wait in the Azul Room." Dancer swept aside curtains of metallic beads and showed them into a lounge that lived up to its name. Cobalt velvet. Sapphire blossoms. The ceiling a holograph of cerulean skies, cotton-white clouds floating through the room. Crystal strands hung like rain drops, twirled like dancing girls, scattering light over the mirrors that floated on the walls. A guaranteed migraine.

"Have a seat." Dancer gestured to the small round table in the center of the room.

"See that she's punctual. I'm a busy man. And I'll pay extra."

Dancer smiled. "I wouldn't insult her, if I were you."

Since when was paying double an insult? But female intuition was at a dire premium these days, so perhaps she could afford to play the diva.

"Go to the bar and pretend to have a drink." He

waved Stilton away. For what he needed to say, Fairfield didn't want even synthetic ears prying.

"But, sir," Stilton objected.

"Go." Fairfield pointed. And took some satisfaction in Stilton's disappointment. The ultimate satisfaction would be the day Fairfield deactivated him. A quick click to the neck, no warning or reason given. Fairfield never explained himself. Besides, hybrid synths were prone to begging when faced with death. It was far easier to put a reassuring palm on the back of their neck, and then *click*, data wiped, battery draining of life.

Fairfield startled when the silver beads parted, and a woman slender as the stem of a peony entered. A dress of thinnest silk kissed breasts piqued like the small beaks of sparrows. Fairfield could buy whatever synthetic he wanted. But not this. Something intangible in her that sparked desire. A trick of pheromones no doubt. Synthetic ones never got it right.

"So, you're the Fortune Teller. You're late. I expect my appointments to be kept."

"Me, the Fortune Teller? Hardly." The woman set down a glass holding a bare inch of liquid the color of dragon fruit, frosted with silver. It moved and glowed in the glass. The latest thrill. Cocktails that adapted to the chemistry of your mouth, gave you a high like no other.

"I only drink martinis." He pushed it away.

"It's the most expensive cocktail we have, Mr.—?"

"Smith."

"We get a lot of Mr. Smith's at Dancer's."

He watched in dull embarrassment as a holograph screen leapt to life between them, flashed his face, then "Fairfield Hughes" underneath.

"Mr. Hughes." The waitress retreated to shaded disdain. "I'm surprised they let you in here."

A wave of nerves came over him. He gulped the cocktail down. The liquid was cold, then warm, then seared his throat. He coughed and hacked as it coated his lungs. "I'm..." He sucked in air, wheezing.

"Can't find a breath? Karma is alive and well, then." The waitress turned on her embroidered heels and left the room, which was beginning to undulate. His stomach felt like he was diving through the skyways again, like he was going to vomit.

"I understand you're a tril-Hex'er," a smooth voice said.

"I am." Fairfield struggled to focus. The singer. The blue top hat. She walked into the room like she owned it, didn't spare him a glance.

"Money won't do you any good here," she said.

"Excuse me?"

"I can't change what I see, no matter how rich you

are."

Fairfield knew a ploy when he heard one, even if he was having trouble getting the floor to stand still. He set ten Hex on the table, enough to keep the Dragon Room running for a year.

She raised her hand. From the ceiling a moonstone orb floated into her palm. The colors moved in reaction, deepening to amethyst. Walking to the table, her hips were wielded as weapons, the shortest of blue skirts riding up past her garters. That sinister black silk smirked at him. When she set the orb down on the table, it didn't roll, stood perfectly still.

"My fee is a par-Hex. Not ten large."

"Well, take it anyway. Get yourself a new skirt. It's evident you can't afford much fabric." His eyes caught on the plain silver band on her finger. "Maybe buy yourself a dazzler, if Dancer isn't man enough to do it."

She took a lighter from her corset, flicked it to life, and then held it to the corner of the money.

Fairfield quailed. Something was wrong here. Lay a match on a par-Hex, it might smolder, but not flame. Yet, in the spark of a second, the bills bonfired, a queer blue light around them. And almost as quickly, the paper settled to ashes. Ten Hex, gone, all resting on a single, crisp par-Hex, a pittance, not even the cost of a martini at his favorite bar.

"You, you…" Sweat fulminated on his cheeks. There

had been no par-Hex when he set the stack down on the table. Some kind of crass sleight of hand, he assured himself.

"Money won't sway me. A decent man would take comfort in that. I charge a par-Hex out of principle." She folded the bill, slid it between the satin of her corset and the silk of her breasts.

"You have your par-Hex then," he said. "You owe me the future."

She sat, folded one leg over the other, a length of light blue stockings, black heels, those poisonous garters damning his mind. The dimple where the bottom of her thigh met her ass...Fairfield's brain contracted. He wasn't used to such carnal displays.

She placed a monocle over one eye. Resting her elbow on her knee, she balanced the orb on the tips of her fingers and extended it toward Fairfield, as if she wanted it to have a better view of him.

"You have a problem, Fairfield?"

"I assume that's a rhetorical question from a fortune teller. My problem is unique."

"I can see that." Ribbons of light emitted from the orb, snaked around his head. It seemed they were prying into his thoughts. Let them try. His will was stronger than any machine.

"You must be in boiling water to hot foot it down here and ask to see me."

"Someone has shorted me."

"Shorted? I don't understand. Someone gave you the wrong change for your coffee?"

"Someone purchased a 200-Hex contract on the Helio Exchange, betting I will die this month."

"And?"

"And?! Betting against Fairfield Hughes? My father lived to 194. My grandfather, 132. I'm only 60 years of age, in gleaming health, the finest care and food that can be provided man, is mine."

"People bet on everything, on the weather, on sports, on which dog can pee the longest stream, which isn't that far from betting on who will live longest."

"You don't understand," Fairfield said. "I don't expect you would. In a business such as mine, there is no shortage of men coming up beneath me. Men who would relish the chance to make a profit on my demise. The Helio Exchange is several centuries old, the most trusted and respectable place to trade futures. To short me on the Helio Exchange is throwing down the gauntlet, a bald challenge of my authority."

"Yes, but a man in your position is well guarded."

"I am." Never mind that he'd had two attempts on his life this week, both close calls. He adjusted his gold cuff. He wasn't a fool. He had a defense system implanted in his arm. Remove the cuff, and his defenses would go live. Another little flick of his wrist and he could send the Fortune Teller straight to hell. Perhaps he would, if she tested his patience. "I expect I will not die until I'm well past 200. But I'd like your word on that. And I want to know who shorted me. You did a great favor for my friend Morgan Peers, saved him from ruin with your predictions, in fact. He suggested I see you."

"Ah, Morgan." She shook her head. "Just like all the other big boys, driving down here to see their mistresses on the low end, driving huge cars to compensate for a lack of other hardware, if you understand me."

"I'll thank you not to talk like a harlot."

"What a charmer you are. I bet you had it modified, and still can't get a date. I bet all your wives are synth."

Fairfield resisted the urge to cross his legs and hide his abnormally large bulge. His modifications were his own private affair.

"I didn't come here to be abused. Tell me when—"

"You die by your own hand." She ran her index finger around the orb. Little blue lights danced within it. They reflected on her monocle, glimmering.

"By my own hand." Fairfield's gave her a polite, cold smile. "That's not possible."

"I can only tell you what I see. You are dead before you understand that you are dead; your thoughts take longer to die."

"You're wasting my time. Tell me who bet against me."

"It is not one but many. You've hurt many. And they have not forgotten."

"Manufacturing isn't for the weak."

The reflection of blue light in her monocle began to spin. She stared into the orb for some time, her brow clinching. "The leak of 2319 at the Hiyentae plant. You paid a fortune to bury the lawsuits. All those factory workers, Fairfield, and you knew they would suffocate, die gasping for air. The lineal acid, the chemical spill, you knew it would happen."

"*Knew* is a strong word."

"We haven't seen the sun in ten years," she said. "All of us here on the bottom. The cloud layer. A week after the spill, the sky went dark. Acid rain has fallen for a decade. The women, Fairfield. What did it do to the women?"

"Unforeseeable," he hissed.

"You were warned. You had studies done. You knew lineal acid would kill the women, 95% of us lost to ovarian cancer."

"Terrible, just terrible." Fairfield shrugged.

She walked around the table, leaned her rear on the edge of it, right in front of him. Put the tip of her foot on his chair, where his legs splayed apart. The cleavage, real, petrified him and beckoned him at the same time, the blue peppermint swirl in her monocle dizzying.

"How many women are left, Fairfield?"

"Too many," he spat, strung between desire and panic. "Distractions, all of you."

She put her finger under his chin, looked him in the eyes. Fairfield froze, as she ran her finger down his neck, his chest, damnably near the electronic pouch surging in his pants.

"Hughes Manufacturing switched to producing Arnium 5Z," she said. "You charge a king's ransom for the thing we need to protect ourselves against the hell you unleashed on the world. The human race is dying, Fairfield. The hybrid synths have failed to reproduce. Only a few women are left who can. But you made a fortune, hiding in the Hughes Tower, high above the carnage."

"Tell. Me. When," he mumbled, so confused by the competing urges in his head, he'd almost forgotten what he was doing here.

She leaned in close, her mouth hovering near his ear. Too late he realized where her fingers were really going. With a quick snap, she stripped off his gold cuff. His personal defense system chirped three times, going live.

"When will you die?" She twisted his wrist, causing a microscopic needle to fire from his subdermal implant. "How about now?"

The poison needle, meant to be fired at whomever displeased him, instead pierced his trousers and then his own leg. The second the point broke the skin, his heart stopped. But his eyes didn't close.

For a moment he thought he was beyond needing a heart, that he had beaten mortality itself. But his mouth did not respond to the impulse to smirk. Then Fairfield Hughes went dark, crumpled just like any common man. Killed by his own hand. With a little help from Fortune.

"Speed it up, Lyle," Dancer urged, leaning over the ticket desk.

"Tell the synth to sit still," Lyle answered.

"Be nice," the Fortune Teller said. "His name is Stilton. He has feelings."

Stilton sat with his face in a scanner. The ocular map of Fairfield's eyes had been gotten long ago. Ordering a synth to fill those specs and run subterfuge software was certainly not cheap. They'd relied on Fairfield's vanity to pick a synth that looked just like him, not realizing the eyes were not just similar to his, but identical.

"It wants voice recognition," Lyle said.

Stilton put his mouth to the microphone, clicked a subdermal button on his jaw. "Fairfield Hughes. Account X74."

"Your favorite grade-school teacher," Lyle prompted.

"Mrs. Klase," Stilton replied in Fairfield's voice.

"Extraction worked great," Dancer said to the

Fortune Teller, who was only his girl in the honorific sense. She was one of the few chemical widows left from the Hiyentae leak; most had died of cancer. She leaned against the doorway, her data globe downloading all the information it had extracted from Fairfield's mind. Enough to destroy the entire financial sector.

"Routing number," Lyle said.

Stilton rattled it off, then added, "And be quick about it!" with an authentic flair of disrespect that had defined Fairfield Hughes. "Initiate transfer."

Dancer exhaled, as money beamed to one bank account, then ten, then a hundred, a thousand, all of them blinds, exploding in a firework of small detours and altered routing, untraceable.

"You're good at making money disappear, Lyle." Dancer smiled.

"It's not disappearing," Stilton objected. "It's being transferred to the families. Justice will be served."

"Sure, chum." Dancer knew that was true. He also knew the 200-Hex he'd shorted Fairfield's life with, even after it was funneled through a raft of dodges and he paid back his investors, would cut up rather large. Not that Dancer had much time left to spend such money. None of them did. But if this was the swan song of humanity, at least he'd go down drinking Bollinger. And he'd make sure those golden boys in the sky fell hard, hitting every drop of acid rain on the way down.

All the girls in his club felt the same. That's why real women came here, disgusted with the skyway barons, interested in living a little with the time they had left.

Stilton adjusted his glasses. "Ms. Teller should receive a share. After all, she lost—"

"I charge one par-Hex, and that's all." The Fortune Teller interrupted.

"Yes, but—" Stilton objected, his drive for fairness hardwired.

"Don't worry about it, Stilton." Her thumb spun the silver ring on her finger. "Money isn't everything."

It Gets Everywhere

CLICK. CLICK. CLICK.

"Look straight ahead. Smile. The camera is over here. Five, four, three..." He said the same thing, every time, every person, hundreds of them, in the never-ending line. All of them hoping against hope that this would be the year they didn't look like a drunken llama on their driver's license. But Tyler Murray was the prince of petty vengeance, wielder of chainsaws in the Thunder Dome. And he knew to wait a second too long, until the eye drooped, the smile dropped, and the chin fanned out into a bounty of rolls. That was the moment. *Click.*

"Sir, can I take another? This one looks really bad."

"I told you not to blink. You're holding up the line." He gave his final word on the matter, as if holding up the line was a criminal offense.

Then for lunch it was a double cheeseburger, vanilla shake, and onion rings, eaten at his desk. Sure, he could eat in his '98 Honda hatchback. But how much better to survey them all, standing in line, clutching their numbers, sweating, one missing form away from an aortic event. Tyler smirked as melted cheese tangled in his moustache, and greasy crumbs of onion rings jumped onto the paunch under his white button-down shirt. Maybe if he was lucky, Shaniqua Grant would ask him for an onion ring.

Then an hour home in traffic, two if someone was spread like liverwurst across the I-5. Then up three flights of rickety stairs of the apartment complex, his lungs crying for mercy as all 240 pounds of his 5'5" body arrived at the front door of 23B and flung the door open.

In short order, he kicked off his shoes, his feet sinking into brown acrylic carpeting from 1972. Carcinogenic cottage cheese ceilings looming above, he took his belt and pants off, keys and wallet tossed in the crochet trash can that doubled as his man locker. By the time he made it to the floral couch and plumped down with finality, he was in his t-shirt and boxer shorts, reborn and ready for seven hours of training on his gaming system. The Thunder Dome awaited.

There was only one problem.

Kit. His roommate. Named after the car in *Knight*

Rider, sitting in front of the couch in light-blue sweat pants and a "Free Britney" t-shirt, watching *RuPaul's Drag Race.* The coffee table in front of Kit was swamped with fabric strips and his Hello Kitty sewing machine.

"Hi, honey." Kit smiled, one eye perpetually drifting in the wrong direction.

"Don't call me that, dude. Scoot over." Tyler needed to air the boys out, needed a sumo stance to enter Thunder Dome. This was war. There was no place for—

"What is that?" Tyler asked, distracted.

Kit brightened. "It's a quilted toilet lid cover."

"Yeah, okay. But what's on it?"

"Oh, it's a quilted portrait of T-Dog."

If Tyler cocked his head and squinted, it kinda... nope, it looked nothing like T-Dog, the South Central rapper. "Looks like his nose exploded."

"It's a decorative ruffle." Kit flushed.

"I'm not taking a dump with my ass touching T-Dong's face."

"T-Dog. It's T-Dog." Kit went prune purple. "It goes on the lid, not the seat. And it's not for you. I'm sending it to T-Dog as a thank-you for his courageous work for social justice."

"You really think T-Dog is gonna get in his caddy and roll over to Reseda to say, '*Thanks for the quilted toilet cover of my face.*'?"

"Sheesh." Kit pushed his glasses back on his nose.

"You had a bad day at work, I guess."

"Every day at work is a bad day. What's for dinner?" Tyler deployed the master blow of the lord of Thunder Dome. Kit was psychologically incapable of denying a food request.

"Scalloped potatoes with pot roast." Kit stood, skinny as a crochet hook, the twenty hairs remaining on his scalp fluffed and moussed. "And salad."

Tyler curled his lip. "Gross."

"You have to eat vegetables or you'll get scurvy." Kit did his runway swerve to the kitchen.

Tyler swept aside the scraps of T-Dog's face, lifted his game controller, and lit up *Mad Max, Ride or Die.* Tina Turner appeared in her blond pompadour and leather corset.

"You think you're ready for Thunder Dome?" She taunted him with those sultry lips of hers, and he wondered for a minute if Shaniqua Grant would look even better in that outfit.

Tyler's fist clenched the controller. He was ready. This. This was living.

"Sir, can I see some identification?" The cop's voice boomed through the apartment. Kit crouched down behind the kitchen island.

"Yeah." Tyler's stocky frame blocked the door so the cop couldn't come in.

You're my gangsta, Tyler, Kit thought.

"Mr. Murray, we're looking for Christopher Leland."

"Who?"

"Christopher Leland, the legal resident of this apartment. We want to question him in regard to surveillance footage from Michael's craft store."

"Okay." Tyler sounded blank. Kit bent down low and dashed to his room.

"Where is it, where is it?" He faced his ceiling-to-floor shelves that housed his yarns, quilting fabric, and other craft supplies, all organized by color. Taking up six shelves alone, his glitter collection. Disco queen silver, Barbie blush pink, Raja peacock blue, everything from finest grain to large granules. He grabbed the Unicorn Poop glitter he'd gotten at Michaels today and darted to the bathroom that joined his bedroom to Tyler's.

"I can't do it." Kit breathed heavily as he lifted the lid of the toilet and hovered the glitter over it. But the cop's voice was still at the door.

Kit sank to his knees and poured $15.95 of glitter into the toilet. The water glinted and swirled with Unicorn Poop. He reached for the lever and hesitated. How could he destroy something so beautiful?

"What are you doing?" Tyler loomed in the doorway. "You gotta stop boosting shit from Michael's."

"I didn't." Kit faltered. "It's police brutality."

"You're white. You know that, right? I thought Kit was your real name. You actually chose it?"

"What's wrong with Kit?" In his nerves, he flushed. But instead of going down the drain, a glittering sea rose up on the rim and then over. Before he could scramble back, it covered his sweats, the floor.

Tyler picked up one foot as the glitter oozed near him.

"Seriously, that shit is the work of the devil."

"It isn't," Kit sobbed. "It's my bliss."

Tyler's eye twitched and he turned to go back to his game. "Don't forget about the pot roast."

"What did you tell the cop?" Kit called after Tyler.

"That you've been gone the last week knitting socks at your grammy's in Raleigh. They have her name. You better call her, get your story straight."

Kit sniffled.

You lied to the po-po for me. My prince.

"Let me ask you one thing." The mesmerizing eyes of Jock Brazos stared at Tyler. 2:15 a.m. and he'd flicked on the tube to wind down from an intense night of battle.

"Are you evolving?" Jock demanded.

Tyler blinked. "Well, yeah."

"Because if you're not evolving, you're what? That's right, you're dying. Evolve or die. I see you, sitting on your couch, bored with life, overweight, wondering what happened to your dreams. It's not your fault, is it?"

"No."

"Of course it isn't. We all have weak people in our lives who hold us back."

Tyler looked down at Kit, sitting on the carpet by his knee, head flung back on the sofa, snoring, covered in squares of black floral fabric. That was supposed to be T-Dog's hair, Tyler guessed.

"Well, listen to this, you're stronger than all that negativity. You're a warrior. Am I right? Say 'yeah' if I'm right. Louder. Say 'yeah' like a man!"

Tyler's fist curled and rose into the air. "Yeah," he whispered.

"That's right." Jock smiled back, tall and muscular. "You're what? Badass. Say it with me, badass."

"Badass." Tyler mouthed the word.

"And what do badasses do?" The phone number flashed on the screen.

"Ask Shaniqua Grant out." Tyler reached for his phone.

★⭐★

Kit stepped off the lip of the gasping #10 bus, his jacket bulging. He hurried through the alley between complexes, holding back in the shadow and extending his cell phone out and snapping photos in either direction. He pulled his hand back in and checked the photos. No police waiting for him. They hadn't noticed him at Yarn Barn. And why should they? He hadn't been there in at least a week.

He sprang up the stairs, into his palace of peace and macramé. He expected Tyler planted on the sofa at this hour. Instead, he was hopping up and down, his manly accoutrement bobbing along in his boxer shorts. Kit blushed.

"What are you doing, honey?"

"Don't call me that." Tyler panted. "I'm evolving. You wouldn't understand."

"Sure, okay." Kit tried not to stare at Tyler, instead crab-scuttled around the sofa and into his room. Star Buffalo, Black Licorice, and Pam Grier Coffee. As the glitter bottles fell onto the bed, Kit's coat flattened. He had everything he needed now. Everything that T-Dog deserved. What could make his quilt portrait even better? A sparkle in T-Dog's eye, a glow in his cheeks, glitter on his grill.

Kit brought up email on his phone and typed to Tdog_bookings@gmail.com.

T-Dog, I want you to know I shoplifted glitter today. For you. Your biggest fan, K-10.

He pressed *send*. His daily emails hadn't been answered yet. But T-Dog read every one, Kit was sure.

"Don't be weird," Tyler said.

"Why would you say that?" Kit hovered over his toilet quilt with a set of magnifying glasses on as he applied glitter with a miniscule brush.

"Because you're a weirdo." Tyler grimaced. He was down two pounds from eating salad for lunch and an hour of cardio in the evenings. He could feel himself evolving. Sure, it was expensive. But winners know to invest big in themselves. Shaniqua Grant was in his sights. All that stood in the way: Kit.

"I have a friend coming over," he said. "Can you clean this shit up and maybe go out to the craft store for a few hours. I'll pay you, dude. Ten bucks. Just leave for a while."

Kit set his glitter down with the dignity of an exiled monarch, cleared his throat, and looked up at Tyler.

"When is your guest expected?"

"I dunno, ten maybe fifteen minutes."

"Are you taking him to dinner?"

"Her. *Her.* I've been telling you for years, I'm straight."

"I thought you were evolving."

Don't make fun of Jock, don't do it!" Tyler's forehead heated.

"If you're not going to take her to dinner, what are you doing?"

Tyler froze. "I dunno." His plan was to plunder the riches of Shaniqua's cleavage. He hadn't gotten further than that.

"Dunno?" Kip's mouth stretched to a smile that said, *You poor fool.* "I'll set an extra place at the table."

"No, dude!" Tyler's eye pulsed. "You need to leave!"

"It's *my* apartment." Kit rose. "If it weren't for my bad vision, we wouldn't have Section 8 housing."

"Yeah, okay." Tyler had to relent. The $600 he paid in rent was unbeatable, even if he'd had to sign a statement that he was Kit's domestic partner before they'd let him move in.

"What are you going to talk about?"

"We're not gonna talk, dude."

Kit nodded as if this made perfect sense. "You're not feeding her, you're not talking to her. What were you planning to do, Mr. Evolve?"

"We're gonna play Thunder Dome." Tyler was sweating now. He hadn't actually told Shaniqua that.

Maybe she was expecting food. Or worse, complete sentences.

"You really know how to impress a girl." Kit shook his head. "I'll warm up the butter rolls."

"No, godammit," Tyler muttered. "I'll order pizza, just, just don't fuck this up for me."

"It's my name on the lease." Kit shrugged.

Tyler stomped to the bathroom, his stomach suddenly cramping. He pulled out his phone and Googled "Jock Brazos" and "dating." A video popped up.

"Are you a man?" Jock appeared. "Go ahead, I'll wait. Check. You got nuts?"

Tyler looked down. The fact was, he hadn't really seen them in a few years. Too much pot roast and that stupid Kit fattening him up. It was Kit's fault Tyler was single.

A picture of a squirrel flashed on the video, with reproductive organs so big they looked like inflated beach balls.

"What kind of squirrel are you?" Jock asked. "King Squirrel? Or little baby girl squirrel? Do you want these?" The camera zoomed in on the beach balls. "Because you better believe she does. Repeat after me, I am King Squirrel. I am the nuts!"

"I am King Squirrel," Tyler whispered, then flailed at his zipper as his guts liquefied. He sat down in a rush, betrayed by the salad with light raspberry vinaigrette he'd eaten for lunch.

The doorbell threw another jolt of panic through him.

"No, no, Jesus, no." He groaned as he heard Kit answer the door. But that devil salad wasn't done with him. Five, ten minutes he was stranded on the bowl. And when he finally staggered up and flushed, he felt something irritating on his backside, something like sandpaper. His pants were shining. Glitter. From Kit's flushing incident. The stuff was everywhere now, sparkles on the t.p., disco powder on the toothpaste, the mirror looked like Glinda the Good Witch had smooshed her face against it. Tyler pulled up his pants and tried to rub the sparkles off his face. He heard Shaniqua laughing, and Kit too.

"Fuck." He straightened his hair, visualized the squirrel, the beach balls, and opened the door.

"I love the pearl stitch, don't you?" Kit's voice floated over a spread of pork chops smothered in onions and apples. "Great for making doilies, cardigans, all kinds of neat things."

"Me too!" Shaniqua sat like a Nubian goddess at the table. "What's that amazing quilt you're making?"

"Just a little something for T-Dog. He's my hero."

"That's cute. You know him?"

"I've seen him, like, five times in concert."

"My cousin is his security guy."

"You don't say." Kit was glowing.

"Uh," Tyler said. "Hey."

Shaniqua glanced at him, her eyebrow cocking. "You didn't tell me you have a partner. Such a sweetie."

"I—" Tyler froze. A fleck of glitter fell from his hair like a scarlet letter.

"Honey, you're sparkling." Kit smiled. "Dinner is getting cold. Sit down."

Tyler sank into a chair.

"After dinner, Tyler plays that little game of his." Kit waved toward the TV. "You know how boys are. But I can show you my craft shelves. And there are brownies for dessert."

"Sure." Shaniqua nodded, and gave Tyler side eye that said by 9:15 tomorrow, all of their coworkers would know he was the smallest, girliest squirrel in the forest. They weren't beach balls, they weren't even walnuts or peanuts. They were little flecks of glitter now.

"I don't just play Thunder Dome," Tyler objected.

"Oh, that's right. He likes to watch Jock Brazos. You heard of him?"

Shaniqua frowned. "That jerk? How many lawsuits does he have against him? Every woman in L.A. is suing him for sexual harassment."

"Girl, tell me about it." Kit nodded. "Toxic masculinity. Like we need more of that."

"He's expensive too. What, two grand a month for

his 'coaching' skills?"

"Pass me the pork chops," Tyler muttered.

"I thought you're on a diet." Kit's eye glistened with revenge. "I made a salad for you."

Kit leaned over to Shaniqua conspiratorially. "He's trying to lose weight."

"Aren't we all, honey!" She laughed. "Pass me those butter rolls. I'd love to see your craft room, Kit."

"Oh, call me K-10."

"K-10. Like *kitten*? You're too cute!"

Kit wheezed, doubled over as the door slammed behind him. Somehow the security guard at Craft Shack had known.

Kit had been careful, waited until there was a spilled paint bottle on Aisle 12 and a baby shrieking at the register before he slid the glitter into his coat pocket. T-Dog was almost done, Kit just needed Dusty Rose fine grain #5 to give his upper lip a little sparkle. And Kit didn't have $7.55 to buy it. Section 8 meant he had just enough to keep the table set with pot roast and pork chops, all the things Tyler liked. Kit was a vegetarian, but he still profaned the flesh of cows to keep Tyler happy. But since Shaniqua had come ever, Tyler had skipped dinners and locked himself in his room with his game system and the TV. Kit could hear Jock Brazos booming under the door. Something about squirrels.

How had the guard known to stop him? Kit had mentioned Craft Shack this morning, when he reminded Tyler to drop the rent envelope off at the front office.

"I already did it a few days ago," Tyler had grunted. "Besides, why should I be the one to do that? You have nothing to do all day except hang out at Michael's."

"Craft Shack," Kit had said. "Today it's Craft Shack."

"Whatever," Tyler had muttered, but then relented. "I can drop you there on my way to work."

An olive branch. Or so it had seemed. Until that security guard tried to run him down.

Kit went to his room to put the bottle of Dusty Rose #5 on his shelf. But where there should be a rainbow, there were only white shelves. His glitter bottles were all gone. Taped to the shelf was a note that said, "If you bring any more of this shit in the apartment, I'm telling the cops to come get you. Shoplifting is for losers."

A knock on the door startled Kit. Security couldn't have tracked him here, could they?

"Kit?" Mr. Willby's friendly voice sounded. "Got a minute?"

Kit composed himself and went to the door. "Mr. Willby, nice to see you. Come in for coffee? *General Hospital* is on."

"Oh, not today." The man smiled. "Just wanted to see about the rent. Not like you boys to be late. Everything okay?"

Kit felt queasy. "I'm so sorry, Mr. Willby. Tyler... Tyler didn't drop it off to you?"

"Nope. And I'm here every day."

Kit heard the echo of Shaniqua Grant saying it was two grand a month for Jock Brazos's coaching services.

Kit made his excuses to Mr. Willby and retreated to the couch with Dusty Rose #5 and T-Dog.

You stole my Benjamins. Trashed my glitter. And called the po-po on me. How could you, Tyler?

Kit sat there, like a milky-faced Geisha in front of the sofa. Not in jail. Tyler threw his wallet in the crochet trash bin so hard it toppled over. He stripped off his pants, imagined beach balls inside his boxers, and claimed his two-thirds of the couch.

Kit was dusting T-Dog's lips with...glitter. Bile boiled in Tyler's throat. He'd thrown out 216 bottles of the stuff this morning. And he'd called Craft Shack to tell them a girly bald man in house slippers was going to steal glitter. Yet. Here was Kit with more of the shiny shit.

"What's for dinner?" He scowled and reached for

his game controller.

"Broccoli," Kit said, the glitter brush starting to quiver.

"Broccoli and what?"

"Just broccoli. It's economical." Kit continued dusting that rose abomination on T-Dog. "Mr. Willby stopped by. You must've forgotten to give him the rent."

Molten rage flowed through Tyler. "I dropped it off a few days ago. He's getting old, must've forgot." The truth was, he'd spent it on Jock Brazos's upcoming Badass Breakthrough.

"How are we paying the rent?" Kit asked. It wasn't like him to persist.

"Ask your grammy for a loan. Not my problem. It's your name on the lease."

Kit colored and said nothing.

"Order pizza, dude. I'm not eating broccoli." Tyler lit up Thunder Dome. Tina was there, sassy, full-lipped goddess of the apocalypse.

"You ready for Thunder Dome, Level 45?" she asked.

He was finally there. Apex predator. One of the few to reach Level 45. Only legends walked this path. Adrenaline surging, Tyler clicked the controller.

Nothing. He clicked again. Nada. Tina was waiting. He clicked two, five times. Then shook the controller. What was wrong with it? Tyler flailed at the battery compartment and flicked it open. An explosion of pink glitter spewed out of the controller, covering Tyler.

"What the fuck is this?" Tyler's voice veered into Mariah Carey territory.

"Glitter." Kit's mouth twitched. "It gets everywhere."

★ ✦ ☆

Shaniqua Grant pulled up to the curb.

"You gotta be kidding me." Her cousin Jesse groaned. "I'm missing a Clippers game for this guy?"

"He makes a good casserole," Shaniqua said, feeling that should end the argument. Kit stood in sweat pants and slippers, something wrong on that little white face of his. He was clutching something in his arms.

She got out of the car. "You okay?" Even in the streetlight it was hard to tell what she was looking at. Kit's face was sparkling pink.

"Thanks for coming." Kit's voice wobbled.

Shaniqua came around the car. Up close she could see that underneath that pink glitter, the corner of his eye had a cut on it.

"It's my fault," he said quickly. "I did something I shouldn't have."

"Uh huh. You know how many times I heard that volunteering at the women's shelter? It's never a girl's faulty, honey, unless you key his car. You key his car?"

Kit shook his head. "Worse. I put glitter in his game thingy. And I made broccoli for dinner."

"Broccoli." Shaniqua shook her head and laughed. "These your things? This all you brought?"

"Yes, ma'am."

As far as she could see, Kit had only brought his Hello Kitty sewing machine and his quilting project. No pajamas or toiletries.

"Jesse?" She tapped on the passenger window. All 6 feet 7 inches of her cousin got out of the car.

"You go on up to 23B and get K-10's clothes for us?"

Jesse looked down at Kit, a question mark rising on his face. "Is that T-Dog on that thing?"

"Looks like you lost." A jovial retiree with nothing but time to wait in line smiled.

"Excuse me?" Tyler lined the man up in the camera's site.

"Looks like you lost a fight with a disco ball." The retiree motioned toward the cast on Tyler's arm. Or maybe he was pointing at the black eye and missing clump of hair courtesy of Shaniqua Grant's cousin. Or maybe the fact that all of it sparkled with glitter that Tyler could not seem to get off himself.

"Five, four, three..." but as long as Tyler delayed,

213

the guy wouldn't break his smile or even blink.

Tyler surrendered. *Click*. Retiree Man waltzed off, well-adjusted, tanned, and soon to receive a license with a photo that made him look like a young Charlton Heston.

Tyler clicked through the afternoon, giving away good photos like they were lollipops. Even his double-cheeseburger lacked satisfaction, then two hours home, I-5 a smorgasbord of lunch meat and smog. Up the stairs. Another letter on the door from Mr. Willby. He tore it off. That's when he saw the box from Brazos, Inc. He scooped it up and hurried inside, chucked the letter next to the others in the crochet trash; he kicked through pizza boxes and In n' Out bags, ripping his pants off. He needed to be in a high state for this. He grabbed Kit's scissors, the ones that said "fabric only" and opened the box. There it was. His XL blue t-shirt with the majestic squirrel, raising his arms as if calling the masses to rise, underneath it, "King Squirrel" in big letters. He struggled to get it on over his cast, his spirits renewed. He picked up his can of air and puffed it at the pieces of his controller, meticulously disassembled. Just another few days and he'd have the glitter out. King Squirrel could do anything. King Squirrel was just getting started.

Without thinking, he called out to the empty room, "What's for dinner?"

★⚹★

"I can't do it, I can't do it," Kit chanted. "I'm just so nervous, Shaniqua."

"You got this, K-10." Shaniqua knocked on the metal bars on the door.

The inner door opened and a short lady in a house dress squinted through the screen and bars.

"You selling bibles? I got one already."

"Mrs. Kravis." Shaniqua pressed her face up to the screen. "It's Shaniqua."

"I know it's Shaniqua. But who's this? He's selling something."

"This is my friend I told you about. He brought his greens casserole."

Kit followed Shaniqua into a home that was covered in ruffles and crochet. It reminded him of his grammy's house.

"Mrs. Kravis, may I compliment you on your star stitch?" Kit said.

"Selling me something," the woman grumbled and led them to the living room. There, sitting on the floral couch, in his bandana and wife-beater, playing a video game with his friend. T-Dog.

Kit's throat went dry. He couldn't remember his own name, much less... "Mr...Mr...Dog. I just...I admire your...your..." Kit's eyes stuck on T-Dog's sculpted biceps. Shaniqua elbowed him in the back. "Your work with inner city youth."

Shaniqua nudged him forward.

"And I...I made something for you."

The quilted toilet cover fell onto the table in a flutter of ruffles and glitter.

"The fuck is this?" T-Dog asked.

"No swearing in this house," Mrs. Kravis snapped, then looked at the gift. "You applique that yourself, son?"

"Yes, ma'am." Kit gleamed.

✫✶✫

"Sir, look up. Sir, look into the camera."

Tyler did not want to. He stood in his King Squirrel T-shirt in the Reseda booking room, for walking out of Best Buy with a new game controller stuck in his cast sling. All his cash had gone to Jock Brazos, including a few months of rent. And the game controller still had glitter gumming it up.

The beefy man behind the camera with a bristly moustache and white button-down shirt seemed vaguely familiar.

"Sir, if you won't look at the camera, Officer Perez will make sure you do."

"I get a phone call," Tyler insisted.

"You got a phone call already."

He'd called Kit, the only number he had memorized, and gotten voicemail. *Welcome to Gangsta Glitta. We're sorry to miss your call. We're currently booking craft workshops for underprivileged youth, funded by private donor.*

It was ridiculous. Kit and Shaniqua's new YouTube channel already had 15,000 subscribers. Just because of one photo. Kit standing between T-Dog and Shaniqua, clutching that stupid toilet cover. Their tagline was "Don't let no one steal your sparkle. 10% of proceeds donated to domestic abuse survivors."

"He didn't pick up," Tyler said. "So I get another call."

Officer Perez moved toward him, then stopped, squinting. "What is that? You been to a rave or something?"

Months later, it was still in Tyler's ears, his nostrils, his hair. No matter how many times he'd vacuumed the couch, it still glittered pink. It had spread through the apartment, and once he was evicted, it somehow found its way into his car and then to his desk at work. That's where he planned to use his new game controller, after everyone else left for the day. Get credit for working late, while he finally, finally made it to Level 45 Thunder Dome.

"Hey, you're holding up the line!" A voice boomed.

Tyler stared. Six feet tall, blue polo shirt that showed off his pecs and biceps. There was no mistaking Jock Brazos.

"What are you doing here?" Tyler asked.

"What's it to you?" Jock looked blank until he saw Tyler's King Squirrel t-shirt. "Just some bullshit charges, man. Be out in an hour."

"Domestic violence," the female cop next to him said. "You're not going anywhere."

"Hey," a man further back in the line yelled, "You owe me money, Brazos. You cancelled Badass Breakthrough and no refunds. I lost two grand on you."

"Yeah!" Tyler nodded vigorously. "All I got was this crummy shirt."

"Talk to my lawyer." Jock shrugged.

"Smile, jackass." Officer Perez grabbed Tyler by the hair and held his face up. Tyler's left eye bulged out, his right one closed, his mouth opened like Mr. Ed at a glue factory, tongue expelled out, all of it glittering with Dusty Rose #5.

Click. Click. Click.

The Hurricane: Mercury in Retrograde

JENNY MANDISI WALKS in a web of light. Spider-fine threads of sensation travel from her, over the parking lot of Loreto Plaza. Above the faux Spanish architecture of stores and restaurants, the palm trees turn to tarantulas in the dusk. Jenny maneuvers around people by estimation of threat, intention, potential pain.

A bald man glances up from an outdoor book table, staring at Jenny's licorice black hair and dress, her spectral face.

"Is that your Halloween costume, honey?"

Jenny is not twelve years old, and this is not her Halloween costume. She is forty. In her Demonia platform Mary-Janes, she crests six foot one, her frame so spindly that she looks like a Gothic pipe cleaner.

A gust of wind whips the pages on the table, startling the man. Jenny slips past him, hurrying to the nondescript glass front of Cherry's Grill, opening the door, and pausing to let her eyes adjust. Framed photos of celebrities hang in uneasy angles on the gold wallpaper. Deep booths of quilted red leather, wagon-wheel chairs, glass lamps. To the left is the mirrored bar, to the back is a moose head on the wall. No moose ever looked so happy to be beheaded, stuffed, and nailed to a wall, overseeing the kitchen doors swinging open and shut beneath his muzzle.

A cadaverous waitress, pinched stomach like a hermit crab, motions for her to follow. Jenny sinks down into Booth #2. From here she can see the whole room.

Jenny casts her lay lines, visible only to her, latching onto the walls, people, the moose. She takes the room in this way. The awkward blind date, an old cowboy looking lonesome in the Gold Room, writers hunched together like ghostly saboteurs at the bar. She judges their distance from her, their capacities, searches for any tremor of instability, and decides the room is as safe as any place can be. She takes off her black messenger bag and puts her phone on the table.

Sorry, late for dins. Rolando's text appears.

When are you not late? Jenny types.

The waitress comes back with bread, and Jenny realizes she hasn't eaten since breakfast. White bread smeared with butter, salsa fresca, and sour cream. Jenny takes a deep bite, smudging her black lipstick, the tomato juice dripping from the corner of her mouth. When she is short of money, sometimes the bread *is* dinner.

There yet? Vanessa texts.

Yes, Jenny replies.

You know the rules. No alcohol.

I'm a grown woman.

If I find you with a cocktail, I will karate-chop you.

Jenny has no intention of obeying her cousin. When the waitress comes by, she orders a Hurricane, the booziest drink in a bar already famed for its slutty pours.

Jenny has another bite of bread and stares at the last text Phil Fleischman sent her.

Great manuscript. The rewrite really works. I'd like to talk to you about printing this.

Jenny feels like she might sail out of her seat, a black-widow balloon filled with helium. After 114 rejections, she finally has a yes. For her book. *The book.* The one she's been working on for years, a manic devotion that serves as friend, lover, and reason for existing. After her nightly shift ushering at the Granada Theater, she threads through midnight streets, the ideas come to her, spinning, spinning. An hour on foot to her rented room in San Roque, and then hours of shadow-dreams dance across her computer screen. She writes a world in which she makes sense, the only place that she does. Except perhaps Cherry's Grill, where tall tales are as common as framed photos of Ronald Reagan.

A feeling like warm honey runs down her spine, pooling in her sacrum. That means Alex is about to text her. She waits, and a second later, a message from him springs up on her screen.

What about artichokes? She hears the text spoken in his voice, a deep amber resin that rolls over her.

Artichokes? Jenny's thumbs fly over her phone. *Death thistles. Prickly, medieval, a rueful food that hides its elusive heart.* And for a second Jenny thinks this describes her as well. She presses send.

So that's a no on artichokes? Alex doesn't eat vegetables. This is a polite exchange of formalities before they decide which end of the cow to eat. *Order me the burnt ends. Thirty minutes out.*

Jenny's heart sinks a little. If Alex and Rolando are both late, that means more time alone with—someone trips her lay lines, a presence behind her, sharp as the snap of a match—her cousin.

Vanessa Mandisi plops down across from Jenny, wearing a white suit and a Tiffany necklace, her ginger hair curled tight like fusilli pasta.

"Rolls is late. Alex too," Jenny says.

"I heard. Drunk driver on 154. Alex had to rappel down the side of a cliff. Whole family of five is toast."

Jenny blanches. Alex didn't mention a cliff or a family of five. But then, Alex rarely tells her anything.

"Do we have to eat here every week?" Vanessa picks up a menu. "Is free bread that sexy?"

"We can't all be lawyers."

"District Attorney. And if I'm footing the bill, I want to pick the restaurant."

"Fine. We can go to Vegan Green. See if Alex will eat Satan tacos."

"Seitan. Sayyy-tawn. Like I care what Alex thinks, Jennifer."

It's not a good day if Vanessa is calling her Jennifer. On a good day, Jenny is Jewels, Vanessa is Vans, Rolando is Rolls, and Alex is still Alex because he won't answer to anything else.

Jenny sees a flicker on her phone, and her adrenaline starts to shimmer. It's a text from Phil Fleischman:

Do you have time to talk about the book? I'd really like to move on it.

Sure, she types.

Great. King's Road?

King's Road is a pub that gets a little rowdy at night. It's already 7. Maybe he means tomorrow.

I like King's Road. She's not sure what else to say.

Great. Tonight, 11 o'clock.

Jenny blinks. There isn't even a question mark after that 11 o'clock.

"What is it?" Vanessa asks.

"The guy from Chapala Press."

"The wiener?"

"Phil Fleischman. Why would you call him a wiener?"

"I see him at the courthouse a lot. Owes alimony all over town."

"I didn't know he was married."

Vanessa's eyes narrow. "What does he want with you?"

"He's considering my book for publication."

"He's considering your ass for penetration, and that's all."

"Your mind is a morass of ugliness."

"So why do you look like someone just stuck a machete in your black heart?"

"He wants to meet at King's Road." Jenny's face heats, although under her zombie-white foundation, it may be hard to tell. "At eleven. Tonight."

"Eleven, King's Road. Sure. Totally normal business stuff. Carry on."

"I'm not his type. I can't be. He drives a Lexus. And wears Italian leather shoes."

"Maybe he collects oddities. Bored, rich guys are like that."

Jenny sees her book in print, a world split open in the hands of others, her life somehow less lonely for it. How badly does she need that? Maybe Phil Fleischman is a nice guy.

"He isn't," Vanessa says, picking Jenny's thoughts

from the air.

"You don't know that."

"I do know it. And I will shit my kidneys out my asshole if I eat any of this." Vanessa slaps the menu down.

"Have a drink then." Jenny's mouth curves. "That's gluten-free. Probably."

"Celiacs is not a joke. Don't start with me. If you think this guy just wants to talk about literature, you are hell and gone from Cartagena, Angel."

Jenny almost smiles. It's a good line. From *Romancing the Stone*. One of Vanessa's few redeeming qualities is her quotes.

"I'll show up," Vanessa says.

"Are you Patrick Swayze in *Roadhouse*? No, don't come. I can handle myself." This last part is not true, and they both know it.

"My god." A deep crease appears in Vanessa's forehead. "Is he another PigSwine McDickFace? You don't like this guy, do you?"

There is a downside to cousins. They know all the dirt. Vanessa has a good memory and therefore good reason to worry. Jenny falls in love silently, glows so violently that she ignites, burns herself to ashes with the pain of the unrequited, and then crawls away, her light dimmed for years after. But she knows who she loves, and it isn't PigSwine McDickFace or Phil Fleischman.

"I look up to Phil, that's all. He publishes good books,

and he teaches great courses."

"Where, city college?"

"Quit talking at me."

Fine, Vanessa changes tactics and *thinks* at her. *It's taken years for you to get your life back together. Don't blow it now on some poser who's stringing you along.*

Quit thinking at me. Jenny clicks her black nails on the tabletop.

Fine. Vanessa gives up.

Jenny checks her phone.

A text from Rolando says, *Bus is late. Almost there.*

A text from Alex says, *Vanessa cheesing you off yet?*

Massive cheese, Jenny types.

There in ten. Order milk.

Now Jenny feels bad she ordered the Hurricane. She usually listens to Alex. Even if he doesn't understand the terms of light and dark that define her world, the way she lifts and tilts and can't find her feet, the way she falls. Still, she listens to him.

I ordered a Hurricane, she types.

DO. NOT. DRINK. IT, Alex replies.

"You ordered a Hurricane?" Vanessa frowns, eavesdropping on Jenny's thoughts. "You're not drinking! I'm still paying Joe's Place back for what you did."

"That was your fault, not mine."

They stare at each other, eyes meeting mid-table in seige. Jenny's fingers curl a little, and the napkin by

Vanessa begins to lift upward.

"Really?" Vanessa raises an eyebrow, and the candle flares. "In public?"

Jenny relents and the napkin stills. Something about Cherry's Grill makes her forget the rules of the mundane world, the imperative to feign normalcy.

Jenny's lay lines jingle. Rolando walks up behind her.

"Hey girls." Rolando is wearing white jeans and carrying a pink clutch on his wrist. He sits with the delicacy of Lady Bird, like he is cradling a bon-bon between his butt cheeks and is afraid to crush it.

"You look like death, Jewels. Something wrong?" Rolando's lips glitter at her. "Wait, you always look like death!"

"It's that guy," Vanessa says. "The wiener."

"Wieners aren't so bad, Vans. Maybe you should try one," Rolando says.

"I'm vegan. And this is guy is a poser. He teaches adult ed, okay?"

Jenny fumes silently, and the edges of Vanessa's hair lift and move like snakes.

Vanessa cocks her head at Jenny. "Leave my hair alone or I will rearrange your doll collection."

"Soooo," Rolando says brightly. "What's the problem?"

"He wants Jenny to meet him at King's Road. At eleven o'clock."

"Booty call, Jewels!"

Jenny's face heats. She doesn't believe in booty calls. She thinks holding hands is a big deal, like a K-O big deal.

"You want this guy to help you, better give him some sugar," Rolando says.

Jenny imagines trying to take her clothes off in front of Phil Fleischman, trying to act normal, like she isn't scared. The edges of her inner landscape darken, time closes in on her, a muddying of what was and what is.

"You're supposed to be the empath." Vanessa flicks Rolando on the shoulder. "Stop with the shit that upsets her."

"You're getting a parking ticket." Rolando smiles.

Vanessa flames her eyes at him. "I don't feel that."

"You parked in a handicapped zone, right? There's a meter bitch out there clocking you."

Jenny's lay lines vibrate. "He's right."

Vanessa springs up and sprints out the door. Rolando unclicks his purse, takes out his tarot deck, and spreads the cards into a fan on the table.

Jenny shakes her head. "I don't want to."

"Pick a card for this guy." Rolando slides the deck closer to her.

"I'll pick the Devil. Or Death. I always pick Death," she says.

"Tarot don't lie." Rolando shrugs.

Jenny sees the card she's supposed to pick. Of course she does. It has the resonance of blue dust hovering above it. Phil Fleischman. She flips it.

Rolando's upper lip curls. "You got the worst luck, girl."

It's the death card, a skeleton cackling and pointing at her.

"Damn it, Rolls. This is my book at stake. Do you know how long I've been working on it?"

"The card's not, like, literal. No one is gonna die... probably." Rolando pulls Jenny's phone toward him. "What did this *chalupa* say anyways?"

She is distracted by the waitress coming to the table. But then she sees that Rolando is typing something on her phone. The trouble with Rolls is he can feel everything, including her password.

"Rolls, no," Jenny hisses.

"Here's your drink." The waitress sets down a massive curved Hurricane glass, glowing pink, topped with a speared cherry.

"What are you typing?" Jenny kicks at him under the table.

"You're not open 24-7, so we're gonna tell him that." Rolando clears his throat and reads what he's typed: "Do I look like a 7-11?"

"No, no, oh my god, no, Rolls, don't you fucking send that!"

229

Rolando's grin dissolves as he catches sight of the Hurricane. "Alex told you not to have no alcohol, right?"

Jenny lunges for her phone and then hears it. The whoosh sound that a text has been sent.

Do I look like a 7-11? Sent. To Phil Fleischman, head of Chapala Press.

Jenny's lungs tighten. A second, ten seconds, a minute, two. There is no reply. Nothing. He is not going to text back. Jenny shoves the straw in her mouth and inhales five shots of rum, vodka, and triple sec. She drinks it so fast her eyes burn.

"He didn't text you back?"

Jenny shakes her head and inhales more booze, her throat napalmed, her brain going thin from the fumes.

Her phone finally pings, and her eyes swan dive onto the screen.

I thought you were more mature than this. Too bad, Phil Fleischman's text says.

Jenny finishes the Hurricane in a numb fog. She wants to spear Rolando in the eye with her fruit toothpick. She wants to run away before Vanessa comes back. And she wishes like hell that Alex was here.

Rolando starts in. "Mercury is in retrograde, that's what it is. Don't say nothing important to nobody—" The fork next to Jenny flies across the table, puncturing the red leather near Rolando.

Rolando side-eyes the fork. "Maybe just don't drink

no more."

But Jenny is not listening to him. She has even stopped drinking. Because she feels something behind her. An energy signature she knows. It's not Alex. And it's not Vanessa. Blue dust and the death card.

Phil Fleischman walks by her booth, wearing camel-colored slacks with a Gucci belt, his hair domed in a pompadour that almost hides his thinning front section. He is putting his phone back in his pocket. He does not notice Jenny.

"Sorry about that," he says. "A writer giving me trouble. You'd be surprised how unprofessional they can be."

"But not me, right?" The woman next to him laughs. She is petite, with soft auburn waves of hair, D-cup cleavage, smiling, well-adjusted. Rita Hayworth in a plum-blue silk dress. Her face is airy and guileless, like gravity has never given her reason to look down.

Jenny watches them sit at a table under the moose head. He pulls out her chair. She places a manuscript on the table. Phil Fleischman was planning dinner with Rita Hayworth at 7, and then drinks with the Goth oddity at 11. She wonders if he is telling Rita the same thing he's been telling her.

Jenny scrambles to salvage any hope of being published.

Sorry, that was a joke meant for someone else, she

texts him.

She watches Phil glance at his phone, the lift of his eyebrows, the cold planes of his face. He taps at his screen. A moment later, her phone pings with his text.

Ok.

Is there ever any hope with an OK?

I can't meet you this evening. But I could have coffee tomorrow, she texts.

Something has come up. Maybe next week.

But the expression on his face tells her there will not be a next week.

Rejection 115 has an air of finality to it that breaks her in a way the other 114 before this have not. Jenny can't breathe. The floor is rotating. She grabs the edge of the table as the pictures begin to rattle against the wall.

"Jesus take the wheel." Rolando slides under the table.

Jenny cannot stop what happens. She tilts off balance, everything blurs, her future churning in lonely spirals that only run parallel to others, never crossing, never meeting. She will spend her life writing in her room, alone. The photos fly off the wall into a cyclone, diners drop their forks, their drinks. Photos of priests and presidents and car salesmen hurtle around the room, bottles of liquor from the bar, Rolando's tarot cards, all converging above the table in the back where Phil Fleischman and Rita Hayworth sit.

There is an inch of air between Jenny's rear end and the seat now. Under the table, Rolando clamps onto her ankles, trying to stop her. Jenny shoves her messenger bag back on, thinking to weigh herself down. But she is unmoored, her lay lines tangled. She is cast into her own storm, floating to the ceiling. Her skirt billows, her hair spreads out around her by centrifugal force, arms reaching for ballast and finding none.

Rita Hayworth screams, looking up as if Jenny is a winged monkey in *The Wizard of Oz.*

"Jenny Mandisi?" Phil Fleischman's voice slices through her delirium. "Is this some kind of stunt? Are you that desperate to be published?"

The drop is like the quiet of high altitude. Freefalling, ground reaching up to sock her in the jaw. The floating photos drop, the bottles too, exploding in a glitter of glass. Jenny lands a few tables away in a heap.

She forces herself up, aware she is bleeding where her legs hit the glass. People are running, limping, and using their walkers to get to the exit. She stumbles to the bathroom, into the stall, sinking to the floor. She stabs at her phone to text Alex.

Please come get me. Bathroom. I'm in trouble.

She searches her bag for the emergency pills. The ones that Dr. Lex prescribes. The ones Rolando calls horse sedatives and says she should slide up her rear for faster effect. But she refuses to try that. Her hands shake as she twists the top, then grinds it the other way, unable to open it. With a pop it leaps off the px vial and a spray of blue pills arc up in the air, clatter off the rim of the toilet, plopping in the water. Her peace of mind sinks to the bottom of the bowl.

Jenny can't breathe, her lungs clamp, her stomach is being hit with a baseball bat. She knows this is a panic attack, but she can't stop it. Her phone beeps and she fumbles for it. She sees a text that doesn't make sense.

We are done, freak.

Alex wouldn't say that. Jenny peers at the screen. Of course she didn't send a text to Alex. Of course not. She sent it to the last person she'd been texting: Phil Fleischman. *Please come get me. Bathroom. I'm in trouble.* After she told him she wasn't a 7-11 and then floated to the ceiling and landed in the glass like Carrie at prom.

There is nothing Jenny can say to fix this. She forces herself to concentrate, to press the call button to Alex.

"Hey." Alex picks up right away. "Where are you?"

"Bathroom."

A minute later, black shoes appear on the tile floor, and the stall door swings open. Still in his EMT uniform, Alex assesses her fleetly, his thoughts undistracted by emotion. "Scale of one to ten."

"Six," she says. As bad as this feels, she knows there is worse.

"Where's the diazepam?"

Jenny flaps her finger toward the toilet.

Alex bends down and picks up the empty bottle, reads the label carefully.

She is embarrassed to be seen like this. She tries to think of something to distract him. "Did you really rappel down a cliff today?"

"Yes." He doesn't look away from the bottle.

"Why didn't you say?"

"You have panic attacks." He checks something on his phone and then opens his med bag.

Jenny sees the silver watch on his wrist, hands steady. She can almost breathe.

"I'm not crazy," she says.

"That is correct." He swabs Jenny's inner arm. "You're psychokinetic, you can't handle alcohol..." He trails off for a moment as he draws clear liquid from a small vial into a syringe. "And you have the worst case of PTSD I've ever seen."

He slips the needle under her skin, finding a vein.

Jenny's teeth stop knocking together. Her chest unclenches. Her lungs sigh. She can breathe again. The baseball bat that has been bludgeoning her stomach stops. Her muscles go soft.

Jenny is like pudding now, unable to censor herself. The honey travels down her spine, filaments of light extend from her, wrapping around him, spinning a space where only they are. She knows that Alex cannot see it or feel it, that he is bound by inscrutable rules that govern him just as surely as Jenny's nightmares govern her. Perhaps this is as close as she comes to another. Maybe anything more is impossible. Still, for a moment she feels safe, feels the solitary core of iron that runs through him, something she can't pierce or understand. She only knows that she comes to ground when he is with her.

Her words leave her easily now. "Rolls took my phone and texted the book guy, the one I told you about. Total disaster. Must be Mercury in...something, I forget."

"Retrograde? Rolando is full of shit." Alex picks up Jenny's phone and scrolls through the screen. "You told this guy you were in trouble and needed help?" The tile under Alex's foot cracks with no warning.

"I thought I was texting you."

Alex scrolls further up the screen. "He wanted to meet you at King's Road. At eleven." The crack in the tile runs up the wall and hits the ceiling.

"I didn't say yes." Her blurred brain can't formulate why Alex is angry. Instead she says, "I'll never be published now. One-hundred-fifteen rejections."

"Just keep writing," Alex says firmly, like he is done with the topic. He lifts Jenny up by the arm, and they move slowly out to the restaurant. She sees a swirl of red leather, broken glass. And Vanessa, blazing with fury.

"You pussy-mouthed mother-fucker!" Vanessa points

a finger at Phil Fleischman.

He is still seated at the table. Rita Hayworth has disappeared. Everyone else has run out. Jenny can't understand why he is still sitting there, except maybe Vanessa is blocking his way. Jenny wonders how her cousin noticed him at all, but then realizes her own thoughts made a map to him that Vanessa could not have missed.

"Have I done something to offend you, lady?" Phil smirks. And it is a really bad idea to smirk at Vanessa.

"How about not paying alimony? How about screwing my cousin over!"

"Your cousin? To whom do you refer?"

"That's it!"

The moose on the wall bursts into flames, its eyes melting, beloved moose smile ejecting sparks. Fur that is over fifty years old burns with an acrid, oily stink. Cocktail napkins erupt into fireworks, the remaining bottles of alcohol go Molotov. A few seconds later, the security cameras light up like Olympic torches.

Phil Fleischman shrieks as the chair behind him starts to burn. His smirk vanishes.

Suspended above him in the air, slowly spinning, is one of Rolando's tarot cards. The death card. Phil Fleischman catches sight of Jenny, and his face mottles. "You! Fucking freak!"

Alex's foot comes down hard on the floor, and it fractures with a deep groan. A seismic shaking cleaves the carpet, the cement, the dirt and stone below. The fracture line shoots straight toward Phil Fleischman's table.

Alex loops his arm around Jenny's chest, like the safety bar on a roller coaster ride, pressing against the underside of her breasts, his palm and fingers under her arm, resting against her ribs. With no warning, Jenny is a million miles away from caring about her book or Phil Fleischman or the brimstone raining down on Cherry's Grill. Joy bubbles in her chest. A floaty feeling tingles in her toes, a sensation of lift.

"Nope," Alex says under his breath and squeezes her tightly, forcing her feet back on the ground. But the bubbles radiate through her, murmuring in a pleasant profusion of warmth. She looks at the scene from a distance. Her asshole cousin wielding fire in her corporate power-suit. Alex cracking the earth in two, pulling a hurricane of a Goth girl to safety. Rolando, the lousiest empath ever, leaking water under the table.

For just a sliver of a moment, Jenny smiles at Phil Fleischman, and she imagines that her black lipstick is smeared on her teeth, down her lips, that she must look like a specter of hell. Maybe she is. And she has friends you really shouldn't fuck with.

"Mandisi." Alex's voice clips the air. "Get Rolando out from under the table. We're leaving. Now."

"Fine!" Vanessa throws her hands up like he's ruining her fun.

Alex pulls Jenny behind him, her legs languid. She watches as the table Phil Fleischman is sitting at slides into the fissure, the fire growing brighter. He claws at the air trying not to sink down with it. His hair-sprayed coxcomb bobs above the floor, and then she cannot see him at all.

The carpet recedes from Jenny's feet, then she feels the smack of night air. The sky is dark now, inky black palm trees reaching for her. She hears Vanessa swearing and Rolando crying. There are police sirens approaching. Fire trucks too. Smoke the color of quicksilver snakes above Cherry's Grill.

Alex deposits Jenny in the ambulance passenger seat and walks around to the driver's side.

"I told you that guy is a wiener!" Vanessa yells, disappearing into her BMW.

"I told you Mercury is in retrograde!" Rolando cries, jogging toward the bus stop on State Street.

Alex starts the engine and shakes his head, eyes crinkling at the corners.

"I told you to order milk."

THE END

Acknowledgements

"Lady of the Lake" was published twice, by *Danse Macabre* and Flatiron Foothills Press.

"Stained Glass" was published by Running Wild Press.

"The First Death" was published in the anthology *The Fifth Fedora*.

"Oh Yes, Dr. No" was published in *Delirium Corridor.*

"Mt. Auborn Danse Macabre" was published in *All Hallow's Eve.*

"The Hurricane: Mercury in Retrograde" was published in *Hurricanes & Swan Songs.*

Follow Silver Webb at silverwebb.com.

www.ingramcontent.com/pod-product-compliance
Lightning Source LLC
Chambersburg PA
CBHW050514260626
47157CB00004B/1315